"Lovely, lying eyes...
like the sea, ever changing,"

James murmured softly across the table to Ria. "Why won't you look at me? You try not to these days, now that you haven't got those phony glasses to hide behind."

Ria lifted her eyes bravely. "James..."

"I'm just asking you to let things develop naturally between us," he said gently.

"I thought you didn't like your secretaries chasing you," she muttered. She knew he was talking about having an affair, and any such relationship would be so wrong for her.

"But you're not," countered James. "Quite the reverse."

"Maybe it's just a ploy on my part," she said desperately, "to trap you into marriage." Surely the word marriage would scare him off, she thought.

Instead, he laughed. "Ria, the day a woman can trap me into marriage is the day they bury me."

SUSAN NAPIER was born on Valentine's Day, so perhaps it is only fitting that she should become a romance writer. She started out as a reporter for New Zealand's largest evening newspaper before resigning to marry the paper's chief reporter. After the birth of their two children she did some freelancing for a film production company and then settled down to write her first romance. "Now," she says, "I am in the enviable postion of being able to build my career around my home and family."

Books by Susan Napier

HARLEQUIN PRESENTS
885—SWEET AS MY REVENGE

HARLEQUIN ROMANCE
2711—LOVE IN THE VALLEY
2723—SWEET VIXEN

These books may be available at your local bookseller.

Don't miss any of our special offers. Write to us at the following address for information on our newest releases.

Harlequin Reader Service
901 Fuhrmann Blvd., P.O. Box 1397, Buffalo, NY 14240
Canadian address: P.O. Box 603,
Fort Erie, Ont. L2A 9Z9

SUSAN NAPIER

the counterfeit secretary

Harlequin Books

TORONTO • NEW YORK • LONDON
AMSTERDAM • PARIS • SYDNEY • HAMBURG
STOCKHOLM • ATHENS • TOKYO • MILAN

Harlequin Presents first edition October 1986
ISBN 0-373-10924-5

Original hardcover edition published in 1985
by Mills & Boon Limited

CHAPTER ONE

ON the morning of her thirtieth birthday Ria Masson studied her pensive reflection. There were faint laughter lines around her mouth and, when she squinted, her eyes. When she lifted her eyebrows more lines appeared on her forehead. There were even . . . she leaned closer to the mirror . . . ye gods! Grey hairs lying among the thick, dark red waves that hung to her shoulders. Her fingers itched to pluck them out but she sternly refused to. She would leave them there to remind herself that she was now a mature woman poised on the downward slide into middle age.

On the other hand, some people might consider that she was just entering her prime. Indeterminate green eyes mocked her vague feeling of depression. She should look on the bright side. Because her creamy skin burned easily she had always protected herself from the sun, so her complexion was still fine-grained and elastic. Her small five-foot-five frame still had a greyhound slimness that bore witness to an energetic life. She had all her teeth, she had her health, and she was happy. What more could a woman ask for in life?

Considering the ups and downs of the last six years, Ria thought she looked amazingly untouched. She wondered what the next six years would bring? Louis? She sighed, getting up from the stool to put on the clothes that she had laid out on her narrow bed. Louis was courteous and kind to the children, but oh, so limited in his outlook. If he had his way she would bloom quietly at his side, fulfilled by the role of wife and mother. But Ria didn't know that she wanted that. She wasn't quiet, not inside . . . she wanted to grab at life as it slid inexorably by, to live it fully, to find excitement . . . fun . . .

She wouldn't find those things with Louis. He was too practical . . . too sensible, and he thought that she was the same. Marrying Louis would be the practical thing, of course. She did have a deep affection for him, and he for her, and she would never have to worry about money again. But there was a price to be paid in something other than cash. She would have to give up her secret dreams, the cherished hope that she might once again fall in love as she had once before . . . swiftly, completely, passionately, intensely.

'Ria!' The harsh bawl floated up the stairs.

'Coming, Paul,' Ria called back, hurriedly smoothing the navy suit and sitting down again in front of the mirror.

'Here we go again,' she muttered to herself as she swiftly dusted her face with powder. A shade darker than her skin, it toned down the freckles which had defeated years of teenage desperation with lemon and oatmeal. Her lipstick was similarly discreet. Next she drew the dark red waves away from her face and secured them in a neat roll. It was like switching off a light, she mused ruefully. Her oval face shimmered with vibrancy when she wore her hair down, but draw away the fiery tresses and everything dimmed except her eyes. She picked up the spectacles that she didn't need and perched them on her small, straight nose. The photochromatic grey of the clear lenses bleached the colour from her eyes, the tortoise-shell frames following a no-nonsense line across her flyaway brows.

'*Au revoir, Mme Masson*, good morning, Miss Duncan,' she grinned to herself, noting with satisfaction the way she appeared to blend in with the blue Laura Ashley wallpaper behind her. Perfect. For the last three years she had performed the same ritual every weekday morning, transforming herself from a warmly attractive woman into a sleek, well-groomed office machine.

Another shout had her grabbing her handbag and dashing down the narrow flight of stairs outside her door. The house, though quite large, was on a narrow section. The whole street was made up of them; detached terraced houses, all weatherboard, all old, but most of them, like Ria's, painstakingly restored by their owners.

The north-facing kitchen was already flooded with morning sun and filled with the spicy smell of warm croissants.

'G'morning, Paul.' Ria gave the short, stocky man by the stove a kiss. 'There's no need to keep bawling at me you know, I can tell the time.'

'Then why is it you're always running late?' came the gruff reply in lightly accented English. 'If you didn't have two built-in alarm clocks I don't think you'd ever get out of here in the mornings. Your coffee's getting cold.'

Obediently Ria sat down at the kitchen table and sipped the milky offering. 'Well, I didn't get any wake-up call this morning. Where are they?'

Paul Masson turned and gave his daughter-in-law a twinkling smile from under bushy grey eyebrows. The gleam in the dark brown eyes told Ria he wasn't a bit fooled by her nonchalance. She was piqued because no one had wished her Happy Birthday yet. Ria blinked innocently back at him, falling in with the game as she watched him limp to the oven and pull out a couple of croissants, splitting them open and placing them on the table in front of her. A weatherbeaten man in his late fifties Paul looked exactly what he was ... an ex-merchant marine. After spending most of his life as a ship's cook on board French vessels one might have expected him to have fixed ideas about a woman's place in life, but Paul had risen gloriously above the chauvinistic attitudes of his countrymen. He had appeared out of nowhere when Ria had needed him most ... and had stayed. Because of his leg injury he could no longer serve at sea nor hold down any strenuous job but he had taken over the running of the household with alacrity and provided a firm hand with his grandsons. Ria had long since stopped feeling guilty about the role reversal. She had realised quite early on that Paul was truly in his element pottering about the house, handling the small renovation tasks, exercising his Gallic charm on the local housewives at the supermarket and creating his heart out in the kitchen.

Ria picked up the jam spoon and took the lid off the ceramic dish of plum preserve.

'Hey, what's this?' Instead of the rich red jam there was a small, gold-wrapped package.

'Happy Birthday, Mum!' Two giggling figures burst out from behind the kitchen door and inundated her with hugs.

'I wondered when someone was going to remember. Is this a new kind of jam?' she teased.

'No, it's our present.' Two voices spoke at once and two pairs of dancing brown eyes watched her inspect the package.

'What's in it?' Ria shook it hopefully next to her ear.

'Guess?' ordered the sturdy little boy on the right.

'No, don't guess, open it and see,' corrected the equally sturdy boy on the left.

'Don't I get a kiss as well as a hug, first?' asked Ria.

As usual, Jamie was first while Michel patiently awaited his turn, informing her gravely, 'We really should be giving you thirty kisses, but that would take ages.'

Chuckling, Ria accepted a kiss from Paul over the identical silky black heads.

'I know I'm getting old, there's no need to rub it in.'

'You're not *that* old,' offered Jamie consolingly. 'Andy Peterson's mother is *thirty-five*.' He sounded awed.

'Goodness, one foot in the grave already,' said Ria, taking the compliment in the spirit in which she was sure it was offered. She half-regretted her flippancy when she saw the boys exchange a giggle. No doubt they would repeat her remark to Andy, who would repeat it to his mother. Six-year-olds could be excruciatingly honest at the most inappropriate of times, as Ria had discovered to her embarrassment more than once.

'Come on, Mum, open it,' urged Michel, hopping from one foot to the other.

Ria pulled at the wrappings. Last year the boys had given her a rather crooked vase which they had laboured lovingly over in their school hobby class. It was at times like this that she longed to be able to turn to René and share with him the acute pleasure of parenthood. But René had barely known his sons. He had been critically injured in a car accident only two months after their birth and had died several weeks later without regaining consciousness. Over the years the intense pain had dimmed to a gentle ache. Her sharpest regret now was that he would never know that his sons had grown up in his own image, a double image, with dark hair and eyes, strong little bodies and all his capacity for love and affection. Of the two, Jamie was the most like his father in character—happy, eager for experience and extremely bright. Michel was more retiring, more pensive, but no less willing to tumble into mischief with his brother.

'Oh darlings ... they're beautiful,' Ria breathed as she unfolded the tissue in the tiny box to reveal a pair of delicate ceramic ear-rings ... tiny blue flowers perfectly fashioned. Ria had had her ears pierced several weeks ago and was looking forward to replacing the gold sleepers with just such delicacies.

'*Grand-père* helped us,' said Michel scrupulously. 'We hadn't saved quite enough. But *we* chose them.'

'They're lovely, just what I wanted,' declared Ria holding them up to her ears. 'The best birthday present I ever had.'

'Don't forget the cake, we're going to have cake tonight. *Grand-père* made——' Michel clapped a hand over his brother's mouth before he could betray the secret.

'I won't, I promise. I won't be having dinner with you because Uncle Louis is going to take me out, but

I'll be sure and have some delicious cake,' Ria promised. 'Now you two hurry up and have your breakfast or you'll be late for school, thirty kisses or no.'

'They're not the ones who are going to be late,' said Paul, looking pointedly at the kitchen clock. 'Sometimes I wonder how you keep that job of yours when you're so disorganised around here.'

'It's because I know I can rely on you, *mon brave*,' said Ria as she prepared to leave. 'I'm so organised at work that I love to come home and relax into mild incompetence. 'Bye everyone. Have a good day.'

' *'Voir, Maman*,' chorused the boys, already quarrelling cheerfully in French about who was to have the window seat on the bus. It never ceased to amaze Ria how easily they slipped from English to French and vice versa. She spoke French fluently herself but it still took a mental adjustment to switch languages. Of course Paul had spoken French to the boys right from the start, and still did, having realised that once the twins started school it would be very easy for them to lose some of their bilingualism.

Ria had to run for her bus through a sprinkling of warm summer rain but she needn't have bothered. Halfway through the fifteen-minute journey it broke down and all the passengers had to be transferred to another bus. It was at times like this that Ria missed having a car, but the expense was still out of the question.

René would have been appalled if he had known the problems he had left behind him. His accident had occurred on a trip to Los Angeles and because there had been evidence of his drinking beforehand his insurance company had refused to pay the full amount of the horrific medical bills that had mounted up in the five weeks he was in intensive-care. All their careful savings had gone on paying Ria's fare to L.A. and accommodation for her and the twins. Alone in a strange city with two tiny babies and a dying husband it had been like a miracle when Paul turned up. She had never met him, knew that he and René had seen little of each other since René's mother had died when he was eighteen, at their home in New Caledonia. But suddenly he was there, a rock, supporting her against numbing grief. Unfortunately he had been unable to help her financially and she had been forced to sell home and car to pay the bills. Even then she still owed a great deal, and, back in New Zealand, despaired of ever struggling free from the crushing debt-load. Social Welfare payments helped with day-to-day living expenses but Ria wanted more for her sons than just the basics.

Paul had accompanied her back to New Zealand and for a while helped supplement their meagre combined incomes with part-time jobs. He liked New Zealand and had no compelling reasons for returning to New Caledonia but at his age, with his disability, Ria felt it unfair to lay upon him the burden of breadwinner. By the time the boys were two they had worked out the solution. Ria would work while Paul looked after the twins at home. A top-flight secretary before her marriage and pregnancy, Ria could command high wages ... particularly in the lucrative temping jobs. Gradually the situation had eased but only when she had got her present position had things markedly improved. About the same time a lottery win had provided the deposit for the house they now lived in in Ponsonby and Ria had grimly plodded from bank to bank to find one willing to lend to a woman, a widow and mother. Her money worries weren't entirely over, but all the old debts were finally settled and there was light at the end of the tunnel. In a few months the mortgage would finally be paid off and she could think about buying a car.

'Morning, Miss Duncan,' the security guard called out to her as she crossed the foyer of the Plaza Building in downtown Auckland.

'How's the new grandchild?' Ria broke her stride to ask.

'A darlin'. She's being christened on Saturday. They're calling her Farrah.' The man's ruddy face showed what he thought of his daughter's choice and Ria laughed. The guard thought, as he often did, that it was a shame Miss Duncan didn't laugh more often. She was a real lady. She should be married, with children of her own to laugh with, instead of working like a slave for that demon on the fourteenth floor. 'Your boss is back. Passed through here like a blue streak half an hour ago.'

'Oh dear, my holiday's over then.' Ria smiled at him as she went over to the lift. James Everett had been away for three days and she had welcomed the breather.

No sooner had she sat down at her desk than the intercom in front of her buzzed impatiently.

'Are you there yet, Miss Duncan?' came the rasp, just as impatient.

'Yes, Mr Everett.' She picked up her pad and pencil and walked through to the inner office without knocking. It was twice as large as hers, furnished in the same blues and greys, but far more lavishly. Everett Communications took up four floors of the Plaza with its head offices and advertising agency but this office was where the buck stopped ... and this was the man who stopped it.

He didn't look up at the sound of her entry, his dark head bent over a report on his desk.

'You're late.' It was a statement, not an accusation, and it was wrong, but Ria didn't bother to correct it. It was still only eight-forty-five a.m. and she wasn't supposed to start until nine, but usually she was in the office before her boss and since James Everett assumed that her whole world revolved around him it was a natural mistake for him to make.

'Where's Gerry?' he demanded, his aggressively beaky nose still buried in the report. It was his nose that stopped a handsome man becoming a beautiful one, for the rest of his face, heavy lidded and full-lipped, was undeniably attractive. He was a smash with women and

Ria felt genuinely sorry for the ones who ignored the warning of that jutting nose and fell for the misleading beauty of the rest of his features. They all lived to regret their mistake.

'I don't know. I've only just arrived.' She barely got it out before he snapped:

'Find him.'

Expecting courtesy from J.E. was like expecting pigs to fly. Ria went back to her desk and rang through to the office down the hall.

'Morning Tracey, is Mr Crane in yet?'

'Just on his way,' the girl answered and Ria relayed the information to her boss, who grunted.

Ria sat quietly, waiting, watching. Her eyes fell on the grey sideburns where they swept up into a jet-black hair. Why, he had more grey than she and he was only twenty-nine. It amused her to think that she was older than her boss. In terms of worldly experience she was probably light years younger. He had a physical and mental toughness that many people, even men, found intimidating and the harsh lines of maturity scored on his face made him look older than his years. The square-cut jawline was hammered out of steel and the ice-blue eyes, now lowered under thick black lashes, could chill a volcano at fifty feet. Ria was thankful that she had never felt a spark of personal interest in the man. She knew him too well to find him as irresistible as other women did ... she had been too well forewarned.

Actually his impatience, his surliness in the office, his extreme wariness of female staff had been a godsend to Ria. He set high standards, but as long as everyone lived up to them he asked no questions. His respect, once gained, was never lost and he backed his subordinates to the hilt against outside threat. His hard-bitten attitude was understandable. James Everett had come up the hard way. A drop-out at fourteen, he had spent several years on the streets before lying his way into a job which had provided the basis for his current wealth.

Like boss, like secretary, thought Ria with an inward grin.

'Morning, Miss Duncan, morning, J.R.' Ria turned to nod at the blond, blue-eyed giant who sauntered into the room.

'Don't you think that joke's worn a little thin?' snapped the man behind the desk, looking up at last.

Gerry Crane shrugged his athlete's shoulders and took a seat beside Ria. Officially designated as J.E.'s right-hand man his good humour hid an off-beat intelligence.

'Anything you say, chief.' He angled a sidelong grin at Ria. Whatever the boss's opinion, most of his employees used the TV character's nickname. They were all pleased to be working with him rather than against him. Ria had seen grown men come out of his office looking shaken, all the more unnerved by James Everett's habit of becoming quieter in inverse proportion to the rise of his rage. 'We missed you. Another few days and the whole place would have come apart at the seams.'

'I doubt it,' J.E. leant back, steepling his hands. 'Miss Duncan kept me fully informed by telex and you seemed to be handling things very efficiently.'

Ria settled down to half-attention as the two men discussed several problems which had arisen with the ad agency budget. Her mind wandered to the first occasion, three years ago, when she had listened to their conversation ... only that time she had been eavesdropping.

She had been lunching at a city coffee shop after visiting the secretarial agency to let them know she had finished another temporary job.

When the two men walked in she recognised James Everett immediately. As the owner of several magazines, two radio stations and a film and video production company he kept a high profile in the media. Coincidentally, she had only that morning heard his name mentioned at the agency.

A young woman at the office had complained about her interview that morning at Everett Communications.

'I didn't even get to first base,' she grumbled. 'The people in personnel told me I was too young. Mr Everett apparently likes his secretaries mature. Mind you,' she lowered her voice, 'maybe I had a lucky escape. Why do you think he's looking for someone outside his organisation instead of promoting? Because they all know what he's like, that's why!'

'Oh?' Ria murmured cynically, having had a problem with an over-eager employer only a few weeks before. 'Does he expect his secretaries to provide extra-curricular services?'

The other girl looked at her as if she was mad. 'Are you kidding? That dish! It's the reverse. All his secretaries fall like ninepins and end up leaving in floods of tears 'cos he's not interested. He treats them like dirt. I tell you, Torquemada isn't in it, according to my friend in personnel! Apparently . . .' she lowered her voice still further so Ria had to duck her head to hear what she was saying, '. . . apparently two of them made real trouble for him. He made a rule about only having married secretaries, and *they* were the worst of the lot. One got all bitter and twisted and spread some nasty rumours and the other one made a terrible scene in the office. Her husband made all kinds of threats. So now it's no married women.'

'That lets me out,' said Ria drily. Not that she would be interested. She earned good money temping. Most of the top-paying secretarial jobs involved long and erratic hours. They were for dedicated career women, or ones with an eye to the main chance, rather than someone who wanted to spend as much time as possible with her family. Idly she added, 'I suppose the money is good though, if you want to work all hours.'

'Probably fantastic,' the girl agreed. 'But actually, the hours were great. Strictly nine to five, Monday to Friday and no overtime.'

'Really?'

'He apparently has this incredible old biddy working at his place. Been his live-in secretary for years and does all his overtime and away trips. World War One vintage, I hear, so no threat to his bachelorhood. I ask you, who can compete with a loyal old biddy?'

'So why doesn't he just shift her into his office?'

The girl tossed blonde locks. 'I suppose even she can't work twenty-four hours a day. Then he'd be stuck with finding someone else for home.' She grinned slyly. 'Imagine the stampede ... every masochist in the city would be panting after the job. He'd be worse off than ever.'

Ria had felt sorry for the poor man. From her experience in offices she knew how tortured relationships could get when they crossed that fine line between business and personal lives. If James Everett had had a string of bad luck with his secretaries it was no wonder he wanted someone mature, someone who didn't see the job as anything more than a job.

She watched as he and his companion walked over to seat themselves in the next banquette to Ria's. Yes, she could see where some women might find that faint air of cruelty attractive, a challenge. He looked like a man who had lived hard and paid for it.

She had been able to hear their muffled conversation through the padded walls of the booth and listened without compunction. The warm lazy tones must belong to the big blond man because the harsh, rapid-fire speech could only be Everett's.

She was just preparing to leave when her ears picked up the intriguing: 'You'll have to make a decision soon. You can't go on indefinitely with a series of temporary secretaries. Another week and you'll have cleaned out the building!'

'I'm damned if I'm going to risk another fiasco by settling for second-best.'

'What's the matter with the ones you've seen so far?'

'Too much thigh down below, too much mouth up

top.' The acid contempt burnt Ria's ears. 'Not to mention what's palpitating in between.'

'It's your reputation,' came the lazy chuckle, 'only the most brazenly ambitious dare apply. Why don't you try a male?'

'In this country they're as scarce as hen's teeth. And the ones I've seen have paid too much attention to muscling up the ladder. I don't want a trainee executive, I want a shorthand typist.'

'Maybe if you treated your secretaries a bit more like human beings and a bit less like robots——'

A short, barking laugh. 'Then what happens? They think they have a right to involve me in their boring little lives, and try to invade *my* privacy. Why should I have to waste time pandering to their egos? My God, you'd think the amount I'm willing to pay would be appreciation enough . . .' He named a sum that had Ria doing a few quick mental calculations. Why, that would mean she would be able to pay the mortgage off in three years instead of five! She listened harder.

'So describe to me then, J.E., this paragon for whom you have been scouring the city. What would she be like . . . other than technically qualified?'

'Quiet, efficient, unobtrusive——'

'Sexless.'

The flat cynical voice picked up without a beat. 'I *was* going to say: not pretty enough to be a distraction, not plain enough to seethe with spinsterish fantasies. Loyal, trustworthy, obedient without being servile. Someone. who won't panic in a crisis, who won't pout when I criticise her work, who won't rush off to get married or pregnant at the drop of a hat.'

No wonder he was having trouble finding her, thought Ria. If he did she'd be wearing a halo and wings.

'And how do you expect to uncover all these sterling qualities in a single fifteen-minute interview?'

Ria held her breath, an idea taking strong root and needing this knowledge to grow.

'I heat the kitchen.' In her mind's eye Ria could see the slightly cruel smile that would be on his lips. 'If they can take it without melting they're halfway home.'

'And the other half?'

'I kiss the burns.' There was a strangled sound from his companion as the voice hissed on, like the tearing of silk. 'And if they take that, they're out on their backsides.'

'My God, no wonder you have a ninety-nine per cent failure rate. It's impossible. I doubt if a woman exists who could meet those standards.'

'If she doesn't I'll invent her,' came the grim reply.

Or perhaps she'll invent herself, Ria thought, as she slid out from her table.

The next day she had put her plan into action. By-passing her agency she applied directly to Everett Communications and arrived for an interview as the sleek, slightly dull, Ria Duncan. Adding three years to her age she had cleared the personnel hurdle easily and had, another day later, been granted an interview with the great man himself.

As expected he was thoroughly unpleasant, fixing her with a piercing gaze as soon as she set foot in his office, rapping out terse questions which she answered calmly, lying with aplomb.

'You pay well,' she answered when he asked why she had applied for the job.

'If you're expecting it to be a glamour job, forget it. There aren't any perks. No prospect for advancement, no travel, no socialising. You'll be in this office eight hours a day, even when I'm not here.'

Ria had nodded without speaking, not blinking an eye when he demanded that she open her notebook and began firing dictation at an impossible rate.

'I'm sorry, you'll have to repeat that last sentence,' she said quietly as she began to fall behind.

'What the hell are you doing here if you can't make the grade? he snarled. 'I suppose you lied about your speeds to get in here?'

That was one thing she *hadn't* lied about ... he had believed implicitly her story that she had spent the last seven years temping because she had had the responsibility of an invalid mother who had recently died. 'I take one hundred and forty words a minute, sir. But you're dictating much faster than that.'

He gave her an icy stare, as if waiting for her to point out that no one could take dictation at the speed he was giving it. She restrained herself and after a minute he began again. This time she managed to keep up to the slightly slower pace. After she had read it back he didn't bother to comment. He continued his interrogation, and every time that Ria calmly parried one of his gratuitous sneers she felt her confidence grow. She could handle James Everett. In fact, the surly jut of his jaw when he made a thrust reminded her rather of her own Jamie when he was out of sorts. Oh yes, she could handle him.

Although she was expecting it, she still felt a little startled when he changed tactics. He smiled, his face softened and the ice-blue eyes clouded into opacity.

'Do you have much of a social life, Miss Duncan? Any ... *special* male friends?'

'I go out a little but, no, there's no one special.'

He leaned forward, steepling his fingers, leaning his elbows on the polished surface of his desk. 'Good,' he murmured, 'I'm glad.' The ice had thawed completely and his eyes moved over her crisp navy suit in a leisurely survey. He smiled again, invitingly, into her bland face. 'I'd hate to think there was someone else to distract your attention from me.' He paused expectantly but she didn't react. Thankfully she wasn't finding his spurious charm in the least attractive. He wasn't at all like her darling René.

'Perhaps it might be as well if we got to know each other a little better,' he went on smoothly, 'over lunch. Will you come with me, Miss Duncan?' He raised a dark eyebrow, all boyish enthusiasm.

'Is my acceptance a prerequisite to getting the job?'

He tilted his head to one side, eyelids drooping as he studied her cool indifference. 'Would it make a difference?'

'No. Not at all.' Ria waited until she saw the cynical glint in his eye before rising to her feet. 'Thank you for the interview, Mr Everett, but I don't think this is the job for me after all.'

She enjoyed his stunned silence, getting to the door before he stopped her.

'Miss Duncan?'

She turned enquiringly. He had risen, tall and dark against the tinted windows behind him. 'Do you have some objection to lunching in my company?'

'I've worked in a lot of offices over the years, Mr Everett, and I always make it a rule not to get involved with anyone from the company I work for, even on a casual basis. It can cause too many conflicts and complications. I'm sorry, but I couldn't consider working for someone who expected to allow a business relationship to encroach on my private life.'

The touch of weary impatience had obviously paid off. Ria had started the very next week and never looked back. Aware that the first three months were probationary Ria had taken everything J.E. had thrown at her and never once dropped her nerveless façade. He wasn't quite the Torquemada that he was reputed to be but he did believe in testing employees to their utmost. As a matter of self-preservation Ria learned to judge his mood to within a hair's breadth. She knew he was at his most lethal when he was quietest. Like the eye of a storm he could lull people into thinking they had weathered the worst, only to find themselves taken off-guard.

The best way of dealing with his temper, Ria discovered, was to batten down the hatches and ignore it. To soothe him by distracting him with a new problem ... just as she would distract the twins, when they were babies, from tantrums.

The job was like a dream come true. The work

extended her without over-burdening. She could go home every evening and forget about her job until the next morning. There were no pleas to work late, or deal with last-minute business, no need to worry about making a slip since J.E. never asked her about her home life and rarely made a personal remark. After three years they were still Miss Duncan and Mr Everett.

Sometimes, of course, he would exhaust her with his constant demand for perfection and on bad days it took everything she had to stay on an even keel. But it all came out in the wash. She released her tension and frustrations by regaling her family with torrid tales of office conflicts. 'The Beast', the twins had nicknamed her boss, having heard her call him one with reasonable frequency.

After a year she had gained the confidence to relax her astringency a trifle, and leave off the mid-brown hair spray she had been using to tone down her uncompromisingly red locks. Now that J.E. had it fixed in his mind that she was part of the office furniture he wouldn't notice the slight improvement in her appearance. He looked at her but he never saw her, not really, never noticed the way her wide, almond-shaped eyes sometimes glittered like splinters of green glass behind her tinted specs.

'Get the broadcasting file from Miss Duncan before you go, Gerry.' Ria came out of her abstraction to hear the order. 'I want to know what you think Roberts is going to do about the Tribunal's findings. I ran into him down in Wellington yesterday.' Everett Communications was in the race to provide New Zealand's first private television channel, with Edwin Roberts the main competitor.

'Buzzing around the beehive?' grinned Gerry. 'Is he hoping to get some of his old Parliamentary pals into his camp?'

'The old boy network strikes again,' J.E. said sourly. He had worked hard for respect. Ria could sympathise with his resentment against those who had it by mere accident of birth regardless of their worth. 'But I doubt that it'll get him anywhere this time, not if the Tribunal's recommendations are endorsed. Unless he sells his newspaper chain he's not going to get more than a thirty per cent stake in any new channel.'

'I can't help feeling a sneaking sympathy for that wily old bastard Edwin, when I see J.E. get that predatory expression on his face,' said Gerry Crane as he waited for Ria to find the floppy disc in the circular file in the office.

'I'm sure Mr Roberts can look after himself,' she replied. 'He did walk away with *Sailing* magazine just when J.E. was poised to take over.'

Gerry Crane's blue eyes crinkled. 'You know, Ria, sometimes I get the impression that you *like* the boss to fall flat on his face occasionally.'

'Whatever gave you that idea?' she asked innocently. She could relax with Gerry. Out of J.E.'s hearing they were on a first-name basis, and although he was an incurable flirt, he had never tried anything with Ria. Perhaps he didn't want to risk his chief's wrath. Or perhaps he, too, preferred the comfortable friendliness they had established. Within the parameters of the office they liked each other and got on well together.

'Just a certain expression you get every now and then, like now. Overly innocent.'

'Well, it does help to keep his ego down to manageable proportions, even if it plays havoc with his temper.'

'Since when are you afraid of his temper?' Gerry asked. 'You're the only person I know who doesn't duck when J.E. starts chucking bricks. What's your secret?'

'I think of him as a little boy,' she said, impulsively truthful, 'throwing a tantrum to get attention ... and I think of the spanking that's on the way.'

For a moment Gerry looked astounded and then he threw back his head and roared a throaty laugh.

Her intercom buzzed. 'Come in here would you, Miss

Duncan, *if* you can tear yourself away from *Comedy Playhouse*.'

Gerry put up his hands and backed away as Ria grimaced.

'A spanking? Oh Ria, I like that, I really do!' he reached the door, still laughing softly. 'But who would be game enough to mete it out?'

CHAPTER TWO

RIA smiled to herself in the dimness of the car. Louis, an innately courteous man, had already complimented her on her appearance but to paraphrase an old song 'he ain't seen nothing yet'. Wait until she took off her wrap!

Her dress was a drift of sensuous peacock-blue fabric. After sharing a typewriter-shaped birthday cake (courtesy of the middle-aged lady next door who was as good at decorating cakes as Paul was at cooking them) with the boys, Ria had tucked them safely into their beds and helped with the dishes before going to get ready for her birthday date. In a large box on her bed she had found the dress, made for sultry late-summer nights just like this one, the swathed bodice dipping low in front and at the back curving down almost to the provocative dimples at the base of her spine.

Bonne Chance, ma belle, the dainty card read.

It fitted like a glove and Ria had gasped at the image in the mirror. Who was this sexy redhead? She sashayed back and forth, admiring the way the blue seemed to shimmer and slide into blue-green, the way her thigh gleamed through the slit in the side. In fact, she seemed to show a lot of skin all around.

'Like it?'

She had turned to see Paul watching with approval.

'What there is of it is gorgeous,' said Ria, stroking the smooth, slippery fabric. 'But you shouldn't have, Paul.'

'Why not? It's about time you were treated to a few luxury items. You've earned them.'

'Don't you think it's a bit ... er ...'

'It is very *er*,' said Paul, satisfaction creasing the olive skin of his face,' that is why it suits you so well.'

'It'll give Louis a bit of a shock,' she murmured.

'Precisely the plan, *ma belle*. Didn't you say that you wished he'd treat you less like a Madonna and more like an Earth Mother?'

'Well, yes ...'

'And didn't you wish that he would sometimes exhibit a little fire, a little passion in his attitude towards you?'

'Yes, but ...'

'Then, believe me, *chérie*, this dress will light the fire. No man could resist putting his hand in the flames.'

Ria laughed. 'I hope you're right!' Her laughter ended on a sigh. 'Am I being fair to him, I wonder ... to suddenly want things from him that I never wanted before? Maybe it's my age. I have this terrible feeling that life is rushing by and I'm standing still. I love you, I love the boys, I have this house, a steady job and a man who's probably going to ask me to marry him, so why do I feel ... I don't know ... *restless*?'

Paul's brown eyes narrowed. 'I hope you're not just considering marriage with Louis for the sake of it. Don't feel pressured, Ria, do what *you* want to do.'

'But I don't know what I want to do! Only that I want things to change. How I don't know either.' It sounded confused to her, but Paul seemed to understand.

'That's not surprising, Ria. Six years is a long time to be without a man's love. You have devoted yourself to making a home for your sons, that's good, that honours your husband's memory; but now you must start to think *of* yourself as well as for yourself. Just don't fall into the trap of comparing Louis to René ... that would not be fair to either.'

'I realise that, and I'm not, not really.' Ria wrinkled her brow. 'René and I had a wonderful marriage and I'm grateful for the time we had together. Naturally I wouldn't expect things to be the same second time around but that doesn't mean that I should settle for *less*.'

'Well why don't you stop worrying about it tonight and merely enjoy yourself. Come and show your sons how beautiful their mother is before you go. They want to see you wearing their earrings.'

Looking at Louis' familiar profile illuminated by the headlights of on-coming cars Ria wondered if he was capable of bringing her true happiness. He was a kind, considerate man, and he got on very well with the twins, but he had his faults. He was ever-conscious of appearances and some of his autocratic mother's snobbery had rubbed off on him. His home was New Caledonia where he ran a family hotel, though he also travelled extensively acquiring and selling antiques. Ria knew that the boys would have little objection to moving to the romantic South Pacific island, nor would Paul, but did she want to abandon the life she had struggled six years to build to play house with a mother-in-law who barely approved? And at forty Louis was set in his ways. He enjoyed visiting with Ria and her sons, but how would two energetic children fit into his routine? And would he marry Ria without first sharing her bed? Why, they might be sexually incompatible and Ria had enough fond memories of sex to hope that it would play an important part in any future marriage. Louis had never pressed her for any deep intimacy and she wondered why.

Ria sighed. She felt strangely reluctant now, to face the evening. Louis had said he had a special present for her, that he would give her after dinner and all Ria's instincts told her it was an engagement ring. He was going to present it, probably with a sober little speech about understanding and commitment that precluded any passionate outbursts. What would she say? She had given him no reason to believe that she looked on him anything but favourably.

Ria's spirits lifted when she discovered where Louis was taking her for dinner. Usually they dined at one of the better hotels but tonight Louis had chosen a small, candle-lit restaurant which possessed a dance floor and a trio of romantically inclined musicians. It was only a few minutes away from home, but Ria had never been there before. Over the last few years a number of fine restaurants had sprung up in Ponsonby specialising in all kinds of cuisines. Ria wondered what kind they favoured here, the décor being no clue.

She waited until Louis turned to her from greeting the hostess before she took off her wrap. His reaction wasn't all she had hoped. Instead of a shower of compliments leaping from his lips he stiffened. When she turned to give the hostess her wrap she was pleased to hear a slight gasp at the sight of the bare expanse of her back but when she glanced at Louis she had to bite back rueful amusement. It was the young, good-looking waiter standing next to her escort who had made the involuntary sound of appreciation. Louis was wearing a tight expression, his mouth compressed.

As they were lead to their corner table, Ria was conscious of admiring looks and, in one case, a lecherous wink. She smiled serenely and walked on with a smooth, confident sway to her hips. She had forgotten how good it felt to be viewed solely as a desirable woman. Mothers of twin sons were rarely considered sexy enough to attract attention and her Miss Hyde act at the office froze off any interest from that quarter.

As Louis lowered himself silently into his seat, Ria was puzzled and slightly annoyed by his lack of reaction. She knew she was looking as near to beautiful as she ever would be. Wasn't he flattered to think she had dressed up for him? Did the attention she was drawing offend him?

'Do you like my birthday present from Paul?' she asked softly, indicating her dress.

'*Paul* bought it?' He sounded relieved. 'It's very . . . attractive. Not the kind of dress you would buy of course.'

His complacency made Ria bristle. No, it wasn't, but only because she couldn't afford frivolous pieces of femininity. Though her wages were good there had never been enough left over from raising the family to allow for extravagances. If she had the money, why, she would have a closetful of dresses like this one. Ones that made her feel womanly, ones that turned heads and provoked gasps, ones that expressed the individuality she was forced to repress from nine to five each day.

Pique made her smile widely at the young waiter as he brought the menus, and request that he help her with her choice. Classical French, she thought, as she opened the leather folder. Trust Louis. No Lebanese, or Indian adventures for him, just the tried and true. And, she realised, he never looked at her with the open and unfeigned admiration that was in the waiter's eyes. He was usually approving rather than admiring, making her feeling grateful rather than flattered.

The *poitrine de veau farcie*, the young waiter suggested, explaining that it was breast of veal stuffed with mushrooms, herbs and capers.

'Well, if you recommend it, I'm sure it's delicious,' said Ria, giving him a warm smile. 'I'll have that, and the avocado to start with.' She handed back the menu, her green eyes sparkling with pleasure. The soft fabric fell slightly away from her breasts as she leaned towards him and the flustered waiter fumbled the pass and dropped the leather folder on the carpet.

'I'll have the terrine and the chicken breast with camembert,' said Louis curtly, unsettling the poor man even further. 'I don't know why they employ such young, inexperienced waiters,' he complained as their order wended its way to the kitchen. 'His pronunciation was absolutely atrocious.'

'They have to get their experience somehow,' said Ria meekly, hiding a smile. Louis had given his order in impeccable English, a kind of reverse snobbery.

'I'm glad we came here,' she said softly, smiling across the candle-lit table at him. 'It's ages since we've been out on our own. It's lovely of you to want to take the boys on outings but I do like to have you to myself occasionally.'

Louis relaxed visibly, his teeth showing white against his tanned skin. 'I, too, Ria. I'm sorry that I have not had much free time this trip but these travel people are intensely competitive.'

'How are things going?' asked Ria, knowing that he was spending much of his time at the travel seminar negotiating package deals for his hotel.

'Very well. I should say that we will have a very high occupancy-rate next quarter. Your Mr Everett was there one evening, on behalf of his advertising agency. He had a very pretty dark-haired young women with him.'

'About nineteen? That would be Marie Steele.'

'Yes, of course, the shipping line's daughter.' How like Louis to neatly label the girl thus. 'A little immature I thought.'

'She's just shy,' Ria protested mildly. Miss Steele had come into the office several times, which in itself tended to confirm the rumour factory's contention that an engagement was in the offing. J.E. usually kept his private life well away from the office. Ria had never met any of the other women he had gone out with, though she knew, through rumour and media coverage, that there were quite a number. He never asked Ria to send flowers or messages, or make dinner or theatre reservations, or perform any of the other little social tasks that many men expected of their secretaries. Either he did them himself, or, more likely, he got his 'loyal old biddy' Miss Freeman to do so. Ria had spoken numerous times to Miss Freeman over the telephone but relations remained cordially chilly. The older woman had made it tacitly clear that no ambitious secretary was going to enroach on *her* hallowed home turf. Ria, who had now lasted longer than any of J.E.'s other office secretaries, felt like telling her that was the last thing she would do!

'I can't understand why a girl in her position should be shy, not with her background. However, I would have thought her a bit unsophisticated for Everett's taste.'

'Perhaps,' murmured Ria, though she thought Marie might appeal to J.E. for precisely that reason. From what she had seen the girl obviously worshipped the ground he walked on, and maybe a hard-bitten cynic like J.E. needed that kind of unquestioning, undemanding devotion to mellow him. As for being immature, Ria had only been nineteen when she had married and she had been perfectly happy. 'Did you talk to them?'

'Yes, but do not worry, I did not mention you. He was extremely charming.'

'Obviously on his best behaviour,' Ria answered. Louis had never seen the man in a rage—intense, motionless, ripping someone to shreds in that deadly quiet voice.

'What was the occasion?' she asked, anxious to get off the subject of her boss. She had enough of him during the day.

He shrugged, giving her a quick glance. 'A dinner . . . very long and rather boring. You wouldn't have enjoyed it.'

'And you went alone, poor Louis,' she commiserated, wondering about that look.

'. . . Er . . . no, I took someone from the travel agency that handles my bookings.'

'Oh? Anyone I know? asked Ria idly, beginning on her avocado. Nestling in the hollow left by the large stone were succulent pink prawns topped with a creamily sharp dressing.

'No.' Louis was spreading his terrine on to melba toast and Ria was amused by his sudden reticence.

'A woman?' she teased.

'Yes, as a matter of fact. One of the secretaries.' His stiffness made Ria all the more curious. It was most unlike the suave Louis to be evasive.

'Young and pretty?'

'Not very.' He shrugged again. 'Tell me, what did the twins give you for your birthday?'

'These earrings. Louis, have you been dating her?' she

persisted, sensing that if the woman was so unimportant Louis wouldn't be acting so determinedly diffident.

'*Comment?*' He raised his eyebrows, the face under the close-cropped brown hair holding a careful expression of surprise. He'll run to fat in a few years, Ria thought to herself as she noticed the signs of heaviness along his jawline. Louis liked good food and wine and was decidedly unathletic. Ria brushed away the unkind thoughts.

'This woman. Have you been seeing her often?'

He lowered the piece of toast he had raised to his mouth. 'It's not important, Ria, why are you suddenly asking me this?'

Ria wondered herself. 'I'm curious, that's all.'

'All right. I may have a few times,' he said carelessly.

May have? Not very young and pretty?'

'Is she your mistress, Louis?'

'Ria!' Although she had asked the question in a low voice, Louis looked around as if afraid the whole restaurant could hear. 'Ria, this is no place to——'

'Is she?'

Louis was floundering, taken aback by her frontal assault, as Ria rather was herself.

'Ria, really! She's nothing to do with us.'

'I think she is,' said Ria firmly. It seemed very important to get Louis to admit the truth. 'Is she your mistress?'

'I hardly ever see her.' His light brown eyes flickered, and he looked both disturbed and annoyed at having his hand forced.

'But you do, occasionally?'

'Occasionally,' he conceded at last. 'But, after all, I am a man.'

'And I am a woman. What about me? Would you mind me "seeing" another man occasionally?'

'You!' His astonishment was unflattering, and enlightening. 'Ria, what are you saying?'

'I'm saying that if you needed a woman, why didn't you come to *me*?'

If anything he looked more shocked and Ria felt her deepest fears confirmed. To Louis there were two kinds of women: the safe, steady kind that you married, like Ria, and the sexy, exciting kind that you made your mistress, like this unnamed woman. And never the twain shall meet.

Ria was filled with an angry frustration. It didn't so much matter that Louis was seeing another woman, or even that he was making love to her, after all they were not committed to each other yet, but it did worry her that he had obviously never even considered *her* in the light of a sexual partner. Did that mean that if they did marry he would look outside the marriage for excitement, while Ria warmed the home hearth and bore him an heir? It was archaic!

'*Ma petite*, I care for you very much, you know that. I have too much respect for you to treat you lightly. Please, don't spoil what we have over such a silly matter ... and I really don't think this is the place to discuss our feelings.'

For the moment Ria acquiesced but her doubts hardened. She didn't want to be respected, she wanted to be loved, first and foremost. It wasn't too much to ask, even at thirty, was it? Ria noticed he had said *I care*. What a euphemism *that* was. It really meant that, being a cautious man, he had thought long and hard about their relationship and concluded that it would form the basis of a satisfactory marriage. For Ria it wasn't enough. She was suddenly absolutely certain that she didn't want to marry Louis; ever. She had never felt any fierce desire for him, any more than he had felt for her. She violently rejected the idea that she should be willing to settle for comfort and security instead of passion and desire.

The meal was delicious, beautifully cooked and presented and the bottle of champagne a superb accompaniment. As the bubbles tickled her palate Ria determined to enjoy her evening, even though her attitude towards it had changed. She allowed herself to relax, even to flirt a little with Louis, aware that she was being unfair but unable to resist adding to his discomfort. Perhaps she could make him realise that he didn't know her as well as he thought he did. That she really wasn't the kind of woman he ought to marry after all.

Although there were other couples on the dance-floor, Louis made no attempt to join them and Ria wondered incredulously whether he was embarrassed to be seen dancing with her dressed as she was. Granted the dress was a little exhibitionist, but it wasn't actually indecent and it certainly wasn't trashy. Her fingers drummed on the tablecloth as she finished a rum-rich chocolate mousse. As she looked around the restaurant with a restless stare she caught the eye of a young man across the room. He was seated facing her. About eighteen and self-consciously smart in a dark suit, he was frankly staring. Wickedly Ria lowered her eyes and lifted them to give him a slow, seductive smile. To her amusement his face went pink and he actually squirmed in his chair. She shrugged her shoulders slightly and widened her eyes, inviting him to believe that she would rather be anywhere than with the unresponsive man at her own table.

A few minutes later, to her consternation, the young man was beside their table.

'Excuse me,' he cleared his throat and spoke in a nervous undertone. 'Would you mind if I asked the lady to dance?' He looked from Louis to Ria and back again.

'We're just about to leave,' said Louis stiffly. 'I don't think——'

'I'd love to,' said Ria, rising quickly to her feet and taking his arm.

'Uh ... thank you,' he stammered, looking stunned by his good fortune. However, he recovered enough to give Louis a smile which held a touch of masculine triumph. Louis didn't see it, he was too busy looking in annoyance at Ria, his eyes telling her that he thought she was acting irresponsibly.

Maybe she was, but she was revelling in it as she moved into the young man's arms.

'I hope you didn't mind me interrupting,' he said into her ear. He was almost six foot tall and Ria found herself fitting comfortably into his shoulder. Strange . . . it had been almost six years since she had been held close to a firm, young masculine body.

'To tell you the truth I was hoping that someone would.' Ria tilted her head up to give him a warm smile.

'Were you having an argument?' His fingers tightened on her back.

'No. Actually I think he was leading up to a proposal.'

'Prop—? Oh, should . . . would you like me to take you back?' Then, awkwardly, 'Or are you just trying to make him jealous?'

'Quite the opposite,' said Ria wryly. 'I'm hoping I can offend his sense of propriety enough to make him think twice about my suitability.'

'Aren't you suitable?'

She sighed. 'Until tonight I thought I might be, but now I find all sorts of dark, rebellious thoughts seething about inside me.' She could see Louis now, sitting with stiff disapproval at their table. She snuggled closer in defiance. 'Who are you here with?'

'My uncle.' The tanned, boyish face pulled into discontent. 'He's in the middle of reading me a lecture.'

'Oh, what about?' asked Ria sympathetically.

'My friends. He thinks they're a bad influence on me. He thinks I should be concentrating more on my studies.'

'Oh, you're at university?'

His feet faltered slightly. 'Yes . . . er . . . business administration.'

'A potential tycoon, huh?' Ria laughed and he responded with a sheepish grin. 'Are you enjoying it?'

'Yeah, I suppose so, but it's not the be-all and end-all. My parents reckon that I'm not doing as well as I should be. They live up north, Paihia, and I guess they worry . . . not seeing me very often, so they set my uncle on me when they think I'm slacking.'

Ria listened sympathetically as he talked about his friends, to whom his uncle's main objection seemed to be that they didn't have ambitions. Reading between the lines she gathered that her young partner, though bright, was in danger of sacrificing his intelligence to the demands of peer pressure.

'I suppose your parents and uncle are only worried because they care,' she offered gently.

'Huh! My uncle just wants my mother off his back . . . she's a terrible nagger. I don't see that he's in any position to preach, he got into all sorts of trouble when he was young. At least *I've* had no trouble with the cops. But now he's as bad as the rest of them.' Ria heard the note of disillusionment. Uncle, it seemed, had been something of a folk hero before his fall from grace on the side of parents.

'Hey, if you mean the rest of them "oldies" I think I ought to warn you that you're dancing with one. Today is my thirtieth birthday.' She teased him gently out of his frown.

'Really? You're kidding! Uhh, I mean, you don't look it. You look quite young . . . I mean . . . sorry . . .' He was getting tangled in embarrassment and Ria rescued him with a husky laugh.

'Don't apologise, you were doing great. I'm very flattered. I don't think your parents have to worry about you being a success, at least with the ladies! Do you have a girlfriend?'

He shrugged awkwardly. 'I don't get on too well with girls my own age. Anyway, my uncle just told me to forget about women until I've passed my exams.'

'So you got up and marched over to ask me to dance?' asked Ria, tongue in cheek.

'Something like that.' He gave a lopsided grin before he realised that it wasn't the most polite of admissions. 'I mean . . . I was looking at you . . . I wanted to come over but I wouldn't have been game unless . . .'

'Unless your uncle hadn't given you the push. Well, I probably wouldn't have accepted if Louis hadn't been very effectively making me feel like a staid old lady.'

'Staid!' His jaw almost dropped, his blue eyes widening as they fell into her yawning cleavage.

Ria gurgled. 'He didn't approve of my dress, either.'

'Didn't approve!' He gulped. 'I love it. You have beautiful skin.' His palm felt damp on the bare skin of her lower back. Oh, Lord, she hoped she wasn't overdoing this. She had forgotten how little encouragement the young needed.

She turned her bright head against his shoulder and found herself staring into a startlingly familiar face. Ice-blue eyes were narrowed on the way her body was moulded against her partner's, noted the hand straying down her back. Ria's feet tangled briefly. James Everett!

'What's the matter?'

'Nothing . . . at least, it's awfully hot in here isn't it? Shall we go outside for a while?' Not giving him the chance to answer, Ria hurriedly pulled him through the partially opened French doors which led out on to a small terrace.

'Ah, that's better!' She fanned her hot cheeks lightly and moved away over the uneven stones to look up at the velvety blackness pricked with distant stars. She had been silly to panic but it had been instinctive. Of course J.E. wouldn't have recognised her in the dim lighting. And Louis, what would he be thinking of her abrupt disappearance?

She turned. 'We've been dancing all this time and telling each other our problems but we still haven't introduced ourselves,' she said to the shadowed figure alongside her. There were lights concealed in the shrubbery surrounding the little terraced courtyard but they were muted by leaf and flower. 'I'm Ria.'

'Tony.' He shook hands gravely, and kept hold of her slender fingers. 'You're very beautiful.'

'So my sons tell me,' she replied lightly, rescuing her hand. His dismay was instant.

'Sons! But . . . you can't be married!'

'I'm a widow. I have six-year-old twins,' she said firmly, aware now that she had made a mistake bringing him out here.

'I still think you're beautiful,' he insisted, filled with determined male gallantry. His Adam's apple bobbed nervously above his starched white collar. 'Would you . . .? May I give you a birthday kiss?'

'Tony, I'm probably old enough to be your mother,' she said discouragingly.

'I don't care.' He looked half diffident, half defiant, as if he expected a sharp rebuff and Ria felt a rush of affection for his fragile ego. It was terribly flattering to be so pursued after spending the morning worrying about grey hairs and wrinkles. How could it hurt?

'Tony . . .'

Young as he was, he picked up the nuance in her soft protest. Ria felt sinfully wanton as she let him take her rather clumsily in his arms. But his kiss wasn't clumsy, merely inexpert. He made up for it in enthusiasm and Ria found herself curling her arms around his neck, enjoying the sensation of being kissed simply because she was a woman and she was there. She felt the pounding beat of his heart against her breasts and the tension that entered his body with astonishing swiftness. When she drew back he was trembling slightly and she felt a surge of guilt.

'I think we'd better go back in.' She laid a finger across his lips as he was about to speak. 'But thank you for asking me to dance, Tony, and making me feel twenty again.'

'Antony . . . are you ready to go?' The words came with the suddenness of a pistol shot from the half-open doorway. Tony dropped his arms and stepped back from Ria as if he had caught the bullet.

'Uncle James! Uh . . . sure, I'm ready.'

Uncle James. Oh, no! Ria didn't have to look, she

had recognised the voice instantly. Of all the rotten luck!
She draw back, half-shielding herself in Tony's shadow.

'You go on,' she urged him in a murmur. 'I'll come
inside in a few minutes.'

Tony hovered uncertainly for a moment, then after
an impatient sound from the dark outline in the
doorway he muttered an unsteady good night and
accompanied it with a brief hard kiss before re-entering
the restaurant. To Ria's horror, James Everett didn't
immediately follow.

'I think you'd better come in too, your escort looked
on the verge of a coronary when you dragged my
nephew outside.'

Ria bit her lip hoping he would go, but her silence
had the opposite effect. He came down the two steps on
to her level, peering into the darkness.

'Or do you often seduce children in front of his eyes?'

Ria gasped. 'Tony is scarcely a child!'

'Nor is he yet a man. He's only just turned
seventeen.'

Just turned seventeen! Ria was glad that the darkness
hid her horror. She *was* old enough to be his mother!

'*And* still at school.'

A schoolboy! Ria pressed her sweaty palms together
behind her back as James Everett's near six-foot frame
loomed dangerously close. 'We were only kissing,' she
gritted at him, sounding suspiciously like a teenager
herself.

'At his age that's enough, especially with a woman
of your obvious experience. Let me give you some
advice . . .' He was almost on top of her now but Ria
was too busy keeping her head bent and eyes lowered to
listen to what he was saying. She was therefore stunned
when he suddenly reached out and hooked a long arm
around her neck, hauling her against him.

'. . . In future don't use a beardless boy to do a man's
job. If you want satisfaction and your coronary-
candidate can't provide it, choose someone with the
experience to match your own.'

With his other hand he forced her head up and then his mouth was on hers. There was a small explosion at the point of contact. The hard line of his jaw nudged her chin back and up as his hand slid from her throat to her shoulder, and on down her bare back to steady her hips against his. His other hand remained locked under the flowing curls at her nape.

There was nothing inexpert about this kiss. His tongue probed her mouth expertly, the jut of his nose pressing into her cheek and sending the hot whisper of his breath across her tingling skin. As his mouth sank deeper into hers Ria saw the stars whirl above her head and then blank out as her lashes fluttered down and all was feeling. She swayed dizzily closer and his thigh muscles shifted as he took her weight.

He kissed her as if he couldn't bear not to, as if she were the only woman in a world of men, the only one who could give him the pleasure he sought. Ria couldn't ever remember being kissed with such single-minded intensity and it generated heat to her very bones. It didn't matter that he had probably done this hundreds of times before with the same degree of practised passion, for those few seconds he was Ria's alone, and the taste of him totally obliterated the adolescent effort that had preceded him.

His mouth lifted briefly, long enough for him to mutter, 'You kiss like an angel, no wonder Tony looked so dazed.'

Then his mouth enveloped hers again, barely giving her time to draw breath, his teeth biting sensually into her lower lip. Ria shivered, dissolving as she felt the warm fingers of his hand slide indiscreetly under the low curve of silk at her back. His middle finger brushed a tiny, whispering rotation on the sensitive skin where the cleft of her buttocks divided the smooth line of her back. It sent a shooting fire up the length of her spine to where his other hand massaged the hollow at the base of her skull.

It was all over in a bare minute, but when he drew his

mouth away Ria was trembling, rather as the boy had trembled. But Ria was no inexperienced seventeen-year-old to be swept away by the wonder of a kiss. She had known total sexual fulfilment, yet here she was panting as if this was the first time a man had held her in her arms. Sensation still rioted through her as he slowly let her go.

'My nephew and I are indebted to you for an enjoyable end to a rather laboured evening,' he said with softly slurred mockery. He gave a low laugh as she moved restlessly and the light caught the angry green glint of her eyes. He flicked the shadowed valley between her breasts as he drew away.

'And, honey, stick to the big leagues. Corrupting minors is a sheer waste of your talent!'

CHAPTER THREE

AFTER that devastating exit-line it had taken Ria several moments to pull herself together and go back inside; back to Louis. He had suggested they leave immediately and Ria hadn't argued, she was too busy wondering whether her tingling lips were visibly throbbing. It wasn't until Louis switched off the engine outside her gate that either of them spoke.

'Ria——'

'I'm sorry——'

They both began at the same time. Ria continued, 'Louis I think it would be best if perhaps we didn't see as much of each other.'

'Because of Catherine? Ria, she means nothing. It's you I want to marry. It's you I bought this for. You must have known I was going to ask.'

'Oh, Louis.' She looked at the tiny velvet box he had taken from his pocket, blurting out the truth in her anxiety, 'I can't marry you.'

He wouldn't believe her. Nothing she could say would persuade him that she wasn't hurt and offended by his confession that he was seeing another woman. Hadn't she flirted with that callow youth in the restaurant purely out of pique? He was firm in refusing to take no for an answer. He would let her think about it for a while.

'We will have a good life together, *ma petite*. You will see that marriage is the sensible thing.'

Sensible! And he made that remark after a long and completely unstirring kiss. Why couldn't he say something romantic, something erotic. *You kiss like an angel*, why couldn't he say that in a husky, impassioned murmur instead of this talk about sensible marriage? Ria had refused to take the ring but Louis had been soothingly, annoyingly understanding about it, convinced she would come to her senses in time.

The next morning Ria went to work full of trepidation, but her fears proved groundless. J.E. did not leap to his feet on seeing her and point an accusing finger. His non-recognition of her as a seducer of children and corrupter of innocents was total. Contrarily, Ria was irritated at the same time as she thanked God for her deliverance. That blanked-off stare he always turned to her suddenly grated. Last night he hadn't looked at her like that, last night he had *looked*.

As the days slid calmly past, Ria found her irritation increasing. The restlessness she had felt on her birthday didn't abate and to her horror she found herself dwelling traitorously often on how boring her life was and how, briefly, with a kiss, it had been decidedly *un*-boring.

She wrestled impatiently with this new demon. She had worked for three years for James Everett, content to view him as he viewed her . . . as a necessary piece of office equipment. Never, *never* had she thought of him primarily as a man. Now the thought was constantly with her. When orders issued from his hard mouth she found herself remembering the way it had softened on hers. When he signed the letters she gave him she recalled the way those long fingers had trickled down her spine. These memories came slyly, slipping sideways into her consciousness, spoiling the beautiful indifference which which she had previously regarded her employer.

It was a complication that she could do without, what with Louis telephoning her regularly from New Caledonia, pressing her for a positive reply to his proposal, and the unshakeable feeling that each of her thirty years weighed a ton. Who was she? Wife, then widow; Mother; Secretary; Breadwinner? All things to all people . . . but what was she to herself? The answer seemed increasingly elusive. Whatever the answer she was more certain then ever she wouldn't find it in marriage to Louis.

One afternoon, as she sat reading over a completed contract at her desk, J.E. arrived back from lunch with Maria Steele. As she preceded him through the door the beautiful, dark-haired girl pulled a slight face at Ria. Oh dear, thought Ria as she smiled in return, that must mean he's in a mood. But all thoughts of moods, and everything else, faded from her mind as she saw who followed her boss through the door.

'Miss Duncan, will you check my schedule for next week, tell me if I have any away commitments? Don't just stand there, Antony, come in.'

Desperately Ria tried to blend herself into the wall. She was out of luck. The curly brown head turned briefly her way then snapped back in a double take.

'*Ria?*' His face pinkened as his jaw dropped.

'Er ... hello, Tony,' she said weakly, frantically trying to convey her dismay, hampered by the fact that she could only use E.S.P. in front of their surprised audience. She had briefly contemplated pretending not to know him at all, but that might only draw even more attention to the manner of their meeting.

Tony obviously missed the message in her glassy stare. He looked from her to his uncle and grinned. 'Do you——?'

'You've got nothing coming up except the speech at the Independent Broadcasters' Association conference in Christchurch on Wednesday.' Ria cut him off, switching her attention to her employer. As a ploy it was a complete failure. J.E. was frowning slightly, as if young Tony had claimed knowledge of a crime.

'You two know each other?'

'Sure——'

'We met once, very briefly,' stated Ria explicitly, sending Tony a glare that he couldn't fail to interpret, while trying to keep her expression bland.

'Oh, yeah, very briefly,' he said, in such heavily significant tones that Ria nearly slid under the desk.

Damn the boy, he was enjoying this ... the thought of putting one over on his uncle. He was grinning like a Cheshire cat now he realised that J.E. hadn't recognised her. 'I didn't realise that she worked here. The way you talked about Miss Duncan. I thought she was another Freeman.'

'Oh, and the talks with the Printers' Union in Wellington on Friday,' Ria went on grimly, trying to marshal her scattered thoughts while ignoring Tony's grin and Maria's amused curiosity.

'Damn!' Ria had succeeded this time. 'I can't re-schedule either of those. Tony, you'll have to stay at school.'

'I don't want to stay on at school,' said Tony. 'Why can't I just come to your place? I don't need a nursemaid.'

'Don't you?' J.E. rapped, and it looked like a stand-off for a moment, the grimly determined man and the scowling youth.

'Why doesn't he come and stay with us,' Maria said in her gentle, placating voice. 'There's plenty of room and he can come and go as he pleases,' with a smile for Tony, 'and I can keep an eye on him,' with an equally nice smile for the brooding man at her side.

'Come into the office and we'll discuss it,' he replied after a small hesitation. He took Maria by the elbow and guided her towards his door. 'You too, Antony.'

He was quite gentle with the fragile and delicately innocent Maria, quite unlike the James Everett that Ria knew. Could he sustain it indefinitely? she wondered. Had Maria ever seen him in one of his cold rages? Had he ever kissed *her* as if she was the last woman on earth?

'Ria! I couldn't believe it when I saw you,' Tony interrupted her ponderings in a low, rapid voice. 'I thought I'd never see you again. What on earth is going on?'

Ria saw no choice but to tell him. 'Your uncle

doesn't know about the twins ... that I've been married.'

He blinked at her, eyes going once more over her tailored suit and the way her hair was scraped back.

'What is this? Are you in disguise? Are you a spy, maybe, for one of Uncle James' rivals?'

'No, of course not. Tony, you'd better go in or they'll start to wonder.'

Instead he perched on the corner of her desk. He looked younger in daylight, the vestiges of childish plumpness showing under the fluorescent light, where they had been shaved off by shadows the other night.

'Come on, Ria, what's it all about?'

'Look.' Ria shot a look towards the half-open office door. 'He doesn't employ secretaries with families, OK? Especially not solo parents.'

'And the specs? You weren't short-shorted the other night when you looked at me across the room.

'He doesn't employ pretty women, either.'

'He only dates them.'

'Precisely. Now please, Tony——'

'Ah-ha ... so if I spilled the beans you'd be out of a job.'

'And furiously angry,' she agreed.

'Of course I won't tell, Ria, if . . .' He tailed off.

'If what?' asked Ria, humouring him.

'If you'll have lunch with me one day next week.'

'Lunch! Tony! What about school?'

'University.'

'Your uncle said school. Tony, you've only just turned seventeen,' she said severely.

'So, seventeen-year-olds still have to eat lunch.' He didn't seem at all put out that she had caught him out in a lie. 'Where's the problem, Ria? It's just a meal. I really enjoyed talking to you the other night, you know? You didn't talk down to me the way *he* does.'

'No, Tony.' Ria refused to even contemplate it.

'Please?'

'No.'

He got off the desk. 'Then I'll just have to tell Uncle James all about you, won't I?'

'You wouldn't!'

'Oh, yes I would. It's one thing that Uncle James has taught me . . . to go all out when you want something.'

Ria got to her feet, her temper flaring at being held to ransom by a schoolboy. 'How dare you threaten me! If anything, talk like that is *guaranteed* to make me think you're not as adult as you claim to be. Do you always do this . . . run to Uncle James when you can't get your way with mere threats?'

He went scarlet, and hunched his shoulders. At least he had the decency to apologise. 'I'm sorry. I guess you wouldn't be interested in talking to a kid, anyway. Nobody is.'

He looked so forlorn that Ria almost weakened. He must have sensed it because he added eagerly:

'Couldn't I see you one day next week? It's mid-term break, you see, and boarding schools have a week off. My folks are in Australia, that's why I'm supposed to be staying at Uncle James'——'

'Antony?' They both looked up guiltily to the demanding presence in the doorway, just as they had the other night. Oh, God, thought Ria as she saw the brow darken, he's going to make the connection. 'Are you coming through? Or do I take it that you'd be quite happy to stay the week at school?'

Tony obeyed like a scalded cat and for a fraction of a second J.E. remained, staring at Ria. Quickly she bent her eyes to her work, holding her breath until he withdrew.

From the brief conversation she overheard when J.E. ushered out his guests, Ria learned that Tony was indeed to stay with the Steeles for the four days that J.E. was planning to be away. Tony didn't have the chance to speak to Ria again but he mimed a telephone and although Ria shook her head she had the sinking feeling that Tony was a chip off his uncle's block.

Hardly had she recovered from one narrow escape

than she received another shock. Gerry Crane arrived
and was closeted for a few minutes with J.E. before Ria
was summoned.

'Sit down, Miss Duncan—and you can forget the
notebook——' she automatically flicked it open. 'No,
not there . . . there.'

He indicated what was known throughout the company as the Hot Seat. It was placed so that the bright
light from the windows fell almost directly on the oc-
cupant's face, baring every expression to the
interrogator's eyes. Those eyes were fixed on her now
and Ria quelled the urge to swallow nervously. She
received a reassuring grin from Gerry as he lounged
against the desk. So she wasn't about to be hauled over
the coals.

There was silence in the room for a few moments.
Ria concentrated on her breathing. It was a trick she
had learnt in ante-natal clinic . . . to relax the body,
clear the mind . . . it helped one isolate and cope with
the pain of contractions. It was also good for coping
with nerves. While other people impaled on his pitiless
stare fidgeted or smoked, or fiddled with their pens, Ria
just sat, sinking into calmness. It had become a kind of
game with herself, to remain motionless and relaxed
until J.E. gave up trying to make her as hyped-up as
was everyone else around him. That was his game and
as far as Ria knew, she was the only one who refused to
co-operate.

'You must know that for some time Gerry has been
complaining about his work-load,' he began, in a bored
tone of voice that told Ria that whatever it was he had
to say, he didn't want to say it.

Her eyebrows arched slightly as she exchanged
glances with the complainant. Yes, he protested, but he
never failed to do it all. His laziness was all superficial.
He wouldn't be working for Everett Communications if
it wasn't. Those who couldn't cope fell rapidly by the
wayside in this company . . . or were pushed.

'It's crippling me, Miss Duncan,' he drawled

engagingly. 'Not to mention the way it's playing havoc with my private life.'

'I didn't know you had one,' she murmured drily. Gerry had been dating a well-known actress recently and had been making the gossip columns quite regularly.

'I realise, Miss Duncan,' he grinned, 'that you are the final repository of the fine wine created by our fruitful grapevine, but you haven't tasted it all.'

It was true that people often obliged Ria with the juicy details of who was stabbing whom in the back, and who was doing what to whom within the halls of Everett Communications. They knew that Ria could be relied upon to maintain confidentiality, If she thought a certain piece of information ought to be conveyed to the boss the informant could be certain it would be forwarded in a suitably sanitised and anonymous form. It was a two-way flow, for in return Ria issued storm-warning signals that gave those in the pathway adequate time to man the sandbags.

Ria looked back at her boss in smooth enquiry. He was leaning forward in his chair, elbows on the desk, long fingers steepled in front of his face, staring at her with narrowed eyes. To Ria the attitude was disturbingly familiar. He was about to do something he found unpleasant. A faint prickle of warning inched its way up her spine.

'Gerry feels that it's time I made a decision about hiring another executive assistant.'

Ria relaxed slightly. So that was what was annoying him, the thought of having to break in another new face.

'Do you want me to draft an advertisement?'

'No. He's suggested we find someone internally.' His fingertips tapped impatiently against each other, another bad sign.

'Do you want me to inform personnel?'

'No. We already have someone in mind.'

'You want his file, I presume,' trying to work out who it could be.

'Then you presume wrong,' he snapped curtly. 'If you would stop trying to anticipate my every move you might give me a chance to finish what I'm saying.'

Ria felt a prick of annoyance. He *expected* her to anticipate his every move. It was part of her job.

The bombshell, when it came, was completely unexpected.

'Gerry has suggested *you* for the position.'

'Me?' Ria's first reaction was a nervous laugh of disbelief.

'I thought you'd be pleased.' J.E. leant back, his voice laced with cynicism.

The realisation dawned that he was serious, as Gerry explained, 'After all, Ria, you're practically doing most of the job now, and you're quite capable of accepting more responsibility ... you know the organisation inside out. After we find your replacement you can move into the office next to me and share Tracey as your secretary.'

'Naturally there will be a commensurate rise in pay. You'll be on salary and there'll be all the usual fringe benefits,' J.E. added, not taking his eyes off Ria's astonished face.

Ria felt the tingle in her spine turn into something nasty and chilling. Promotion was the last thing she needed—fringe benefits or no. She closed her eyes briefly behind their glass shields. Don't tell me I've been *too* good, she despaired, don't tell me I've perfected my way out of this marvellous niche!

'You seem quite overcome, Miss Duncan,' J.E. drawled impatiently. 'A simple yes or no will suffice.'

He crossed his arms over his chest and stared at his speechless secretary, wishing she'd get on with it. There was no doubt in his mind that she would accept. Only a fool would turn down an opportunity like this and Miss Duncan was not a fool.

Gerry was right, she was wasted as a mere secretary. She had a solid grasp of the essentials of organisation, she was quick to learn and she had an exceptional talent for handling people—even himself. Especially himself. Over the years he had become aware of the skilful way she avoided confrontations with him. No matter what he did she was never ruffled, never argued with him, yet, subtly, she had managed to exert a certain influence in the office. At times, James knew, his temper got the better of him and caused him to act with less than his usual forethought. In the past it had tended to cause complications. Not with Miss Duncan as a buffer. At first he had responded harshly when he discovered that she had muted an angry memo or conveniently 'forgotten' to forward his orders to those concerned. She had accepted the criticism without comment and calmly continued her editing of the worst of his excesses until he had tacitly accepted that she was, in fact, saving him a great deal of inconvenience. Contrarily he sometimes found her eternal damned serenity bloody irritating. It made him feel that it was she, rather than he, who was in control. And how long would it take him to find another like her? He half-wished he had been able to discover some monumental flaw that would preclude him from offering her the new job. Then she would *have* to remain as his secretary.

'No.'

He froze, unable to believe his ears, but one look at his assistant's incredulous expression confirmed the impossible. She was refusing! How dare she reject the offer that he had been so reluctant to give? Didn't she realise he was according her the honour of his trust and respect?

'You're turning it *down*?' Gerry sounded bewildered. 'But, Ria, you can't!'

Ria licked her lips. She could almost feel the thick, gathering clouds over the motionless figure behind the desk. 'Why? Is it compulsory?'

'Of course not, Ria, but for goodness' sake, don't you realise what you're turning down?'

'I think she realises very well,' J.E. said softly, evenly.

'And no doubt she is now going to supply a cast-iron reason why.'

'I simply don't want the job.'

'Come, Miss Duncan,' his voice dropped even further, 'you'll have to do better than that. What are your reasons?'

She looked at the steel jaw, heard the dangerous quietness and felt her stomach heave. What could she say? I don't want the job because I like to get home every evening at precisely five-thirty so I can be with my sons . . . because my family will always, while they need me, come first, even before the almighty James Everett?

'I trained to be a secretary,' she said, stepping extremely carefully through the minefield of attention. 'It's what I want to be. I don't want more responsibilities.'

'Don't you think you can handle it?' A sarcastic challenge that Ria parried with practised ease.

'I'm sure I could, if I wanted to.'

'But Ria——'

Having taken over the interrogation, J.E. intended no interference.

'Perhaps Miss Duncan is inviting us to negotiate.' He tilted forward and laid his hands flat on his desk. 'What is it you're angling for, Miss Duncan? Money? Conditions? Shares?'

'I'm not angling for anything. I do not want the job,' Ria repeated slowly, unable to prevent herself sounding like a kindergarten teacher dealing with a slow child, knowing it was only antagonising him further.

'You disappoint me.' The words dripped ice, tiny cold-tipped daggers. 'I thought you would welcome the opportunity to expand your career. If you're the kind of woman who likes to shirk responsibilities then you shouldn't even be in this office.'

His hypocrisy ignited Ria's rage. After all the effort she had put into moulding herself to his specific requirements! Her body tensed as she tried to control herself, but the urge to fling his hypocrisy in his face was too much.

'May I point out, *sir*, that I have never shirked as your secretary. When I was first employed by you I understood that you required a long-term secretary, *not* an executive trainee. I didn't realise then, of course, that I was to be criticised and insulted for fulfilling the exact terms of my employment. I'm sure, if the situation had been reversed, and I *requested* the opportunity to train for higher office, you would have been shocked and annoyed by my temerity!'

'Uh ... I think she has you there, chief,' Gerry remarked lightly but both combatants ignored him, measuring glares.

'I'm not interested in your hypothetical assumptions. This is here and now. Good secretaries are two a penny, potential executives are not.' The implied insult was infuriating.

'Really?' Ria smiled maliciously. 'Then why is it you had such a difficult time finding *me*? Even good secretaries have trouble tolerating your demands, judging from the lack of applicants for the job.'

A muscle leapt in his cheek. 'You're very eloquent, all of a sudden, in defending your job. Could it be that you have another motive for not wanting to move out of my office?' Ria froze, then flushed angrily as he sneered: 'Could it be, Miss Duncan, that you're harbouring a secret crush on me, and can't bear to let me out of your sight?'

'James——' Gerry was looking from one to the other in dismay, but again he was brushed aside.

'I'm more likely to have a crush on my typewriter, Mr Everett,' she said with all the withering scorn she could muster. 'It has an infinitely more appealing personality. I told you that I didn't want the job and you'll just have to accept my answer as final. If you're going to fire me for daring to want to control my own future, go ahead, but don't try any of your bullying tactics on me, I've seen you in action too many times for them to be effective.'

'The thought of being fired doesn't bother you?' J.E.

shot at her. A new and unreadable expression had entered the cold blue eyes and Ria fought to identify it before she spoke. He should have been more angry, not less, yet his voice had risen to almost normal level.

'Not really,' she said warily. 'I get job offers from people who come through this office quite regularly. Extremely tempting offers. Head-hunting isn't only confined to executives. I turn them down because this job suits me.'

'*I* suit you?' He asked with a mockery that made Ria flare anew. The beast was still trying to imply that she had a crush on him!

'As a matter of fact,' she snapped, 'you're the only drawback in an otherwise perfect job!' She bit her lip as soon as she said it, sure it would bring a return of his lethal quietness.

'A rather large drawback, I would have thought, considering the amount of time we have to spend in each other's company.' Ria tensed her toes, the only part of her that he couldn't see, at his amazing equanimity. It was utterly out of character for him to encourage a subordinate to defy him. Was it because he had decided to fire her anyway?

'So . . .' He rose leisurely to his feet, 'at last, after three years, I begin to find out what you really think of me.'

'I didn't think it mattered what I thought, as long as I did my job,' Ria gritted, rising also so that she would not be at such a disadvantage.

'It does if you're going to work with me rather than simply for me.'

Ria felt dizzy with confusion. So she wasn't fired, but neither was she going to be harassed into doing what *he* wanted her to do.

'But I'm not, I've refused.' Her voice rose alarmingly.

He was staring at her, eyebrows raised suddenly, but at the top of her head, not her face.

'Good Lord, your hair's gone red. When did you do that?'

'I didn't *do* anything, Mr Everett,' she said tartly, feeling that she was balancing on a knife edge. 'I have always had red hair. I always will. I didn't realise I had to have your permission.'

'Then why haven't I noticed it before?'

'Are you calling me a liar? I can prove I'm a red-head.' The irritated words slipped out before she realised how they could be misinterpreted. There was a stifled chuckle from Gerry behind her and J.E.'s mouth relaxed into a curving grin. Ria felt a blush cover her entire body. 'I mean I have photographs.'

'Really?' She had increased his amusement even further and he drew out the first word suggestively. 'Miss Duncan, I had no idea you went in for exotic hobbies.'

'*Baby* photos,' she stressed painfully, her wildly fluctuating colour apparently proving fascinating.

'Ah, of course.' J.E. exchanged a knowing masculine look with his assistant and moved smoothly on. 'Well, now that we have the question of your colouring settled, shall we agree to postpone settlement of the other matter? Take a few days to think about it.'

'I don't need to think about it,' said Ria, totally unbalanced by the embarrassing turn the conversation had taken, and her own stupid gaffes.

'In fact, take a few weeks. There's no need to rush into this. Gerry can cope on his own for a while longer, can't you, Gerry?'

'Sure.'

'I'm not going to change my mind,' Ria insisted.

'OK, but don't let's slam any doors just yet. We'll just let it ride for now.'

'No!' Ria almost wailed her frustration. He was no better than Louis. They both thought that by biding their time they could get their own way, regardless of her feelings in the matter. 'I will not let it ride. I don't want to find suddenly that my personnel file has been re-designated. I don't want to open my pay packet one day and find I've had an inexplicable pay rise. I don't want to arrive for work one morning and find that you've assigned me a "junior" secretary who will gradually take on my work while I take on more and more of G—Mr Crane's. I will not be coerced!'

He heard her out, hands on his hips, the waistcoat of his wine-coloured suit taut across his flat belly. He had been wearing a similar suit the other night, and Ria remembered the way the waistcoat buttons had stamped themselves down the centre of her body, remembered the soft rasp of the fabric against the bareness of her skin. He had had a distinct scent, too, a mixture of sharp cologne and musky male, and Ria's nostrils flared slightly as she detected the merest hint of it now. Oh God, she was losing her mind, thinking of such things!

'How boringly predictable you must find me, Miss Duncan,' he murmured, with a faint acidity that told her her suspicions were confirmed. Nevertheless, his eyes still held a gleam of determination that made Ria wonder what further cunning plans he was making. 'Very well,' he surprised both her and Gerry by saying, 'you have my assurance that there will be no coercion. You will accept the job freely and without reservation or not at all. But I absolutely insist you take the next two days to consider the offer. Agreed?'

He thrust his hand at her and Ria had no choice but to take it. She did, gingerly, and dropped it again hastily as his warm, dry palm slid across hers and set the pulse at her wrist beating uncomfortably strongly.

She escaped at last, conscious of Gerry's reproachful look. Poor Gerry, he had thought he was doing her a favour and she had let him down.

That evening she told Paul of her two close shaves.

'Don't you think that maybe you're laying too much emphasis on his finding out?' he asked as she expressed her frustration. 'After all, you have worked for the man for three years and shown yourself extremely capable. Why should the fact that you have children change that?'

'You could be right,' Ria agreed tiredly, unwilling to wrestle with the problem after just wrestling her two sons into bed and reading them a gruesome tale of monsters and mayhem. 'But I certainly don't want to take any risks until that mortgage is paid off. I came close enough to getting myself fired today just by standing up for my rights; imagine what could happen if he finds out I've been deceiving him for three years? He hates being taken for a ride, in any form.'

'Who doesn't?' Paul commented. 'But surely he would take your length of service into account. You've never had a day off sick so he can't accuse you of absenteeism for the sake of the children. You ought to think about it, Ria, especially if this Tony is going to be the problem you think he might be.'

'Mmmm, yes, I'll think about it,' Ria promised vaguely. Why did problems come in messy lumps rather than in ones and twos? Why did life have to be so *relentless*?

Wretched man! she thought that night as she snuggled down in bed. Who could trust a man who kissed and ran as James Everett did? Kisses and insults, that was all he was good for. And bullying, and conniving, and . . . and . . .

She fell asleep trying to assemble all his faults, all the totally unattractive aspects of his character that would effectively outweigh the unsettling combination of kisses and insults.

CHAPTER FOUR

'WELL, gentlemen, if there are no more comments?'

Ria discreetly laid down her pencil. The tone of voice indicated that James Everett was ordering the meeting closed.

However, this morning, one of the five three-piece suits in the guest chairs spoke up:

'In my opinion the whole thing's a lottery. This is the second submission on private television that we have made and there's no guarantee that, if there's another change of government, we'll not have to start all over again. Television is a fickle business at the best of times. Even if we do succeed we'll be competing against a subsidised state-system. I know we've discussed all this before but I genuinely feel that we're biting off more than we can chew with this one.' Dave Wallford was the company's Finance Director, a conservative thinker who provided a balance for J.E.'s younger, more progressive staff ... and for J.E. himself.

'Short-term losses are inevitable in any new enterprise, you know that, Dave,' J.E. stated, blue eyes dissecting the faces around him for expressions of doubt and aiming his persuasion where he saw it. 'If we don't take risks, we don't get results. Television isn't a new industry. There'll always be scope for our expanded facilities, even if we aren't granted a licence. Our film studios already have more work than they can handle so I don't think we need worry about not meeting our capital costs. In the meantime we have ourselves a tax write-off. You didn't raise too many objections, Dave, to investing in feature films when they provided us with a tax shelter.'

'Hmmph. I did raise *some*, as I recall. And that was

only a matter of a few hundred thousand. This consortium is going to involve millions.'

'Now, Dave, don't go regressive on us,' drawled Gerry. 'Aren't you the same man who persuaded us we needed to take the plunge into computerisation? How many work stations was it at how many thousand per unit?'

'That was a net cash outflow of only six months,' said Dave Wallford, gruffly tolerant of the smiles all round. It was a standing joke that even Wallford himself had been taken by surprise by his sudden enthusiasm for the computer age. He had had to put up with much jocular comment that next he'd be turning up in the office with Superglue and glitter in his hair. 'We had an immediate, concrete improvement in efficiency and it was confirmed in the annual report.'

'Not to mention how much fun you had installing the system,' someone added. 'What's your latest score on Space Invaders, Dave?'

'I appreciate your concern, Dave,' J.E. cut in on the general laughter, 'but we're beyond the point of discussion in this area. It's a matter of policy and the policy has already been decided. How about turning those reservations of yours to good purpose? If you foresee problems, let's foresee some solutions.'

He stood up, indicating the meeting was now indeed closed, and Ria rose too as the men began to file out. J.E. had these meetings weekly. They were a chance for his heads of departments to air their opinions and grievances about anything that affected the running of the company. It gave J.E. a chance to keep his finger on the pulse and his employees the knowledge they had access to the top.

'Not you, Ria. I want to go over these budget proposals one more time.'

Ria was aware of a curious glance or two from the retreating men. Amazing how such a simple thing as a Christian name could provoke such curiosity. The rumours didn't seem to bother J.E., but then perhaps he hadn't heard them. It was two weeks since she had turned down her promotion but still speculation was rife in the building. Common gossip went one of two ways—either J.E. had suddenly become friendly with his secretary because she was in line for a promotion; or they were having an affair.

The former theory was only favoured by those who found the idea of the latter incompatible with their image of the passionless, unflappable Miss Duncan. The slur on her intelligence was annoying, but Ria knew that a statement from her would only fuel the idle speculation. Her only recourse was to act more cool and unflappable than ever.

'Yes, Mr Everett,' she murmured in a neutral tone of voice that she carefully preserved for use in the office.

'Come and sit here beside me, and we'll run these figures through the system.'

Ria moved her chair reluctantly closer as J.E. switched on the small computer terminal at his elbow and entered the program classification followed by his personal code. He tilted the screen so that Ria could see it without strain and then stood to remove his dark blue jacket.

Ria sat, trying not to notice the way the narrow pinstripes of his waistcoat and trousers followed the muscled contours of his stomach and thighs. He hitched his pants and sat down, his knee brushing briefly against hers as he swivelled his chair to face her and smiled pleasantly.

'Ready?' He turned back to open the thick folder on his desk and Ria nervously tried to brush away the slight echo of pressure that lingered on the side of her leg.

They went through the entire proposal, Ria making notes of the adjustments and corrections which, at this late stage, were relatively minor. Months of work had gone into the various reports on Everett's ability to run a regional television channel, and now J.E. was personally assembling the information into a single, impressive, bound and printed edition to be presented at the licence hearings.

'Is something bothering you, Ria?'

Ria's hand, which had been absently massaging her temples, dropped back into her lap as she gave him a startled look. Such concern for her well-being was unheard of!

'Is it the CRT?' He tapped the screen while his eyes studied her pale face. 'Do you find it tiring to use? I know you put in long hours in front of it sometimes. If fatigue is the problem, maybe we ought to run a staff survey.'

Ria relaxed. He was only worried about the wider implications.

'No, I don't have any problems using it. Neither does anyone else as far as I know. I'm just a little . . . tired.' The boys had got sunburnt over the weekend and she had been up and down in the night with cool drinks and calamine lotion. Fortunately the twins had always been very healthy and resilient so disturbed nights had been few and far between since their babyhood.

'Been burning the candle?'

There was no way that was anything but personal. 'No,' replied Ria with impersonal briskness, starting to gather up the papers from the file that were spread out in front of her. Since the day he had offered her that job J.E. had been both subtle and persistent in his attempts to alter the boss/secretary relationship into something more equal. He had even managed cunningly to infer that she was letting her sex down by failing to fall in with his plan to provide women with a greater role in decision-making at Everett Communications. Being totally familiar with his business tactics, Ria had been equally resistant, never giving him the chance to re-open the subject by referring directly to what he was trying to do.

'What do you do in the evenings that makes you so tired the next day? Are you moonlighting, by any chance?'

'Does it matter? As long as I do my job efficiently?'

He watched her hands, small but highly capable, with plain, buffed fingernails, stack up the papers. 'You're being even more evasive than usual this morning, Ria. What on earth is it that you're so anxious to hide?'

'Nothing,' said Ria firmly, realising that she was only intriguing him further by refusing to answer. 'I do housework in the evenings, I like to read late.'

'Really? What kind of books?' He cupped his chin in his hand and leaned interestedly on the desk, as if he didn't have a diary stuffed with appointments at his elbow.

'Science fiction, detective stories——' Ria shrugged 'Chandler, Hammett, that kind of thing,' unable to think of a suitably boring lie on the instant.

His mouth tilted. 'Mmmm, flights of fantasy and the violent confrontation of good and evil. I would have thought you were practical, rather than romantic, in your reading habits.'

'I'm sorry, perhaps I'd better take out a subscription to *Popular Mechanics* so that I fit in with your stereotype of me,' she replied tartly, and was sorry when he laughed, his eyes becoming as blue as the sun-warmed sky outside.

'You're the one who's so anxious to fit into a stereotype. I've already offered you the chance to step outside it.'

'Mr Everett, if you're so damned keen on getting a woman into top management, why don't you advertise the position? Get a woman with the right qualifications and the right attitude.'

'I can't. I'd be prosecuted under the sex discrimination act. Besides, I don't want just any woman, I want *you*.'

'That surprises me,' said Ria, suddenly tired of his fencing. 'It was patently obvious when you were offering me the job that you were doing so with the greatest reluctance.'

He sat up sharply, eyes cooling. At last he felt he was getting somewhere. This was the first genuine response he had had from her in weeks. He had been beginning to think he was losing his touch. Any other woman would have been eating out of his hand by now. But the very qualities that had persuaded him that Ria Duncan would make a good assistant ... not least the businesslike aloofness she always wore ... made her almost impossible to manipulate. She had worked for him for three years yet he still knew next to nothing about her.

Up until now he had not cared. The cold shoulder she had given his generous offer had changed that. He had seriously misjudged one of his employees, and that disturbed him. What else had he misjudged about her? His curiosity, once piqued, fed upon itself. Once he had satisfied it, he could go back to that tranquil, impersonal relationship he had always had with Ria Duncan. Or could he? He looked at the hair dragged sleekly away from her small face. It was quite alarmingly red, seeming to become brighter every time he saw it, especially when the light fell, as it was now, directly across the top of her head. How in the hell had he missed seeing it before? And how in the hell was he going to ignore it in future? All the red-heads he knew were temperamental cats who made the most of their unusual colouring. Why didn't she? And why was she always so damned chilly? The few times he had got a reaction out of her he had glimpsed emotion under tight control. Did she ever relax that control? Was she afraid of her own feelings, or just unable to express them? Had it been a man who had made her the way she was? What kind of man did she go for?

'Is that why you refused?' he probed. 'Look, Ria, I admit that I was reluctant at first ... but only because, as you kindly pointed out at the time, I *knew* I would have difficulty replacing you. I've grown accustomed to your face around here. But the more I think about it the more I'm convinced that it's a waste of talent not to utilise you more fully. Sure, the effort would have to be greater, but so are the rewards ... power, money, influence. I wish you would reconsider, Ria.'

'And I wish you wouldn't call me Ria. Everyone has noticed, and they're drawing all sorts of conclusions.

'The hell with everyone else,' he barked at her. 'You let Gerry call you Ria.'

'Yes, but he's not my boss.'

'But he *is* your superior. What an anachronism you are! Always this insistence on being so terribly, terribly correct.' He put on a Noel Coward accent.

'So have you insisted, up until now,' Ria pointed out tightly. She was finding his combination of intelligent logic, exasperation, and light, almost teasing humour rather difficult to resist. How easy it would be to relax and act naturally with him. She felt the pressure build up in her mind. Paul was right, she should confess all . . . but not yet . . . not yet. And even if she did, she still wasn't going to accept this new job.

'One grows, one changes,' he said softly, startlingly mirroring her thoughts. As the twins grew, their needs were changing, too. What would happen when they no longer needed her? Would she still be satisfied with a limited job, or would she want more when, perhaps, it was too late? 'You can't fight change, Ria. It's as inevitable as drawing breath. What I needed from you three years ago . . . three weeks ago, is different from what I need from you now.'

Fortunately at that moment the telephone rang. The blue phone; J.E.'s private line. He picked it up, motioning curtly to Ria to stay. At the same moment there was a brief knock at the door and Gerry Crane stuck his big blond head into the room. He, too, was gestured in and Ria sighed with relief. Now perhaps the uncomfortable conversation would be averted, if not cancelled entirely.

'Mya? Can't this wait, I'm very——' J.E. was cut off by a loud squawk at the other end of the line. So it was his sister, Tony's mother. With a vague feeling of discomfort Ria turned to Gerry, trying to mask out the one-sided conversation.

'Goodness, where did you get that suit?' she exclaimed softly. 'A little John Travolta-ish isn't it? Is that your actress' influence at work?'

'Don't you like it?' asked Gerry, sliding down into a chair. 'Too flashy, huh?' He looked down at his blinding white suit.

'On you it looks good,' Ria smiled at him, 'though I would say that it's pushing the outer envelope of the company's policy about dress.' The executives were expected to wear suits and ties the year round but Gerry, acutely clothes-conscious, prided himself on free interpretation of the rules.

'All right! But just remember that I haven't got time to solve *all* your family problems for you!' Ria turned her head to catch J.E.'s frown as his eyes flickered from Gerry's grin to her faint smile. She wondered what his sister was saying to annoy him so much, and was dismayed when she found out a few seconds later.

'Trouble at t'mill?' Gerry asked facetiously as the receiver crashed down.

'My damned nephew again.'

'If this is personal——'

'Sit down!' There was a brief silence as Ria subsided and James tried to control himself. 'I'm tired of you always sidling out on me. A few personal insights aren't going to contaminate you, for God's sake. If you can bring yourself to tease Gerry about his actress you can damned well sit there and listen to *my* problems for a change.'

'Been truanting again, has he?' asked Gerry delicately while the other two measured stares. 'Your sister was worried about some glue-sniffing friends of his, wasn't she?'

Glue-sniffing? Ria was appalled. Tony was in far worse company than he had led her to believe.

'Glue-sniffing I could handle, the boy's got brains when he cares to use them. No, the scent he's on now is even more malodorous, according to Mya's fevered imagination. Tony, it seems, has entangled himself with an older woman. Much older, says Mya, a widow, and French to boot.'

Ria nearly fell out of her chair. What on earth had Tony been saying?

'*Cherchez la femme*, huh?' grinned Gerry. 'Or is it the black widow?'

'I think that's what Mya has in mind.' James scowled at the telephone. 'He went home this weekend and did nothing but rave about this incredible woman he had met. Laid it on thick enough to worry Mya, then clammed up when she tried to find out the details. Naturally she blames me. But, dammit, he's not *my* son. If he was he wouldn't even be at that so-called "progressive" school. All he really wants is attention— and Mya and Ken should be supplying that.' He slammed a hand down on the desk. 'God preserve me from adolescent infatuations!'

And how, affirmed Ria silently. She should have realised this might happen. 'You be careful, Ria,' Paul had warned when Tony had haunted their house during his mid-term break. 'You may think you're only making him welcome, but you're probably the first older woman he's been around who's not a member of his own family, or a friend's mother. He's at an awkward stage with girls, but you make him feel comfortable and at ease. He might easily convince himself that this is a special relationship.'

Ria had listened but been sceptical. On the surface Tony seemed so pleasant and un-intense. There had been none of the complications she had feared when she arrived home from work the first day J.E. was away during the mid-term week, to find Tony sitting on her garden wall.

He had sprung up at her approach. 'Ria! Hi.'

'Tony! What are you doing here? How did you find out where I lived?'

'I did a bit of sleuthing around Uncle James' office,' he confessed airily.

'You should have rung first. I might not have been coming home,' she said severely.

He swallowed, brashness faltering. 'I thought you might not have let me come.'

'You knew I wouldn't. I don't think this is at all wise, Tony. What if your uncle found out?'

'He won't care.'

'But I would. Does Miss Steele know where you are?'

'I said I was going to a friend's. She's having people over to dinner so she's going to be too busy to entertain me.'

'In other words you lied.'

'I thought you *were* my friend,' he replied, so mournfully that Ria, although she knew she was being manipulated shamelessly, melted.

'How did you get here?'

'Bus,' he said eagerly. 'The Steeles only live round in Herne Bay. I could even walk here.'

Ria sighed. 'You'd better come in. Just for a short while, though.'

'Sure.'

Of course, it hadn't been a short while. He had stayed for a meal and watched television. At first he was stiff and uncertain with Paul and the boys, but once he dropped his attempts to act like a sophisticated adult he fitted easily into the little family circle. When he was getting his own way he had a natural, likeable charm, so that it was easy to forget who his uncle was.

The next evening the same thing happened, except this time when Ria arrived home Tony was already inside, sitting in the kitchen peeling vegetables. Paul gave Ria a tiny, silent shrug.

'Tony, you shouldn't be here. You're wasting your mid-term break. You should be out enjoying yourself.'

'I am enjoying myself,' he retorted firmly.

Ria contemplated her choices. She could ask him to leave but she was aware that he was suffering the pangs of homesickness as well as the rebellious stirrings of adolescence, and that the two were incompatible in his mind. He had told her that he was going to help his mother and father in their boat-building and chartering company in Paihia when he had finished a business course at university. From the way he talked, Ria knew he was quite keen, but that he also somewhat resented the way his life was laid out in front of him, was tempted to turn his back on it and try something completely new. No wonder his family was worried about the company he was keeping. At this delicate stage in his life he was very vulnerable to peer pressure, eager to experiment. Ria knew she shouldn't encourage him in a deception but she decided that there was less harm in him spending time with her and the twins than hanging around the streets or video parlours with his friends, bored and looking for excitement.

So she let him make the most of his week's holiday, stressing only that he was to give Maria Steele Ria's phone number, so that she would know where to contact him. J.E.'s return hadn't stopped his visits, but the resumption of school had, and Ria had been relieved. Now she was aghast to hear that he had so built up their brief friendship in his mind that he could speak to his parents about her. Thank God, he had apparently showed *some* discretion. Was it just another way of flaunting his indepedence in his mother's face . . . or did he genuinely have a crush on Ria? Naturally her sympathies were entirely with his mother!

Luckily J.E. was distracted from his dissertation on the trials of unclehood by pressure of work, but Ria went home that evening extremely uneasy at the thought that he might be going to do some investigating into Tony's mystery woman. From his remarks it was apparent that his parents feared not only an emotional entanglement, but also a financial one. Tony had a considerable inheritance from his paternal grandfather falling due to him on his eighteenth birthday. Remembering the small gifts of toys he had bought for the twins in spite of her objections, and the flowers and chocolates he had given her, Ria felt a fresh wave of guilt. From the outside perhaps it would look as if she were vamping the poor boy, instead of just extending the hospitable warmth and friendliness that flowed naturally from the Masson household.

Having got into the habit of pouring out his troubles into Ria's receptive, uncritical ear, Tony had taken to telephoning her sometimes from his school. Usually Ria was quite happy to spend a few minutes chatting to him, but tonight when she heard his husky young voice at the other end she forestalled his eager flow of words.

'I don't know what you've been saying to your parents about me, Tony, but I know that you've given the wrong impression of our relationship. I don't like being used, Tony, and I think you're using me as an excuse to annoy your parents.'

There was silence at the other end, then he said truculently, 'I only told them what a great time I have with you. I never mentioned your name or anything.'

'That's not the point, Tony,' she argued. 'Your parents are concerned enough about your progress at school without feeding them a lot of half-truths about me.'

'I didn't, honest,' he cried, hotly aggrieved. 'I *do* like you a lot, I think you're terrific. You never put me down by telling me I'm too young to think this or that, you always listen to what I say and treat me sort of equal. Not like a kid. When I go home Mum and Dad are always too busy to talk about things, but you aren't. You have a full-time job and still have time for your family.'

'Tony . . .' Ria didn't know what to say. At least he was putting her on a level with his mother and father, so even if he was suffering from a crush it was probably as much on her family unit as it was on Ria herself.

'You won't stop being my friend, will you? I promise I won't say any more, I *promise*.' His voice rose urgently. 'I'll be sensible and study and everything, but please let me come around sometimes. I can do lots of things for you . . . I got good at entertaining the twins, didn't I?'

Again Ria had weakened. He was so touchingly eager to be useful, and she felt that it was perhaps only youthful exuberance that had led him to embroider on things to his parents. From now on, though, she told herself as she went for her nightly jog after dinner, she would not be quite such a willing listener ... and his exams were coming up, that would be a good excuse to gently discourage too many calls or visits. It was a pity that his school was so liberal with their seventh-formers ... they were allowed out three times a week to visit approved relatives or friends, and Ria suspected Tony was chafing to acquire himself a new 'aunt' on the approved list. She wouldn't put it past him to forge his parents' signatures as he had seemingly done before when wanting to go out with his friends.

Ria turned a corner at the two-kilometre mark and began to follow the dimly lit route home. She enjoyed running; after sitting down for most of the day it was good to get the adrenalin pumping.

She wasn't sure when she became aware of someone behind her, but when she half-turned, expecting to see a fellow jogger, she instead received a blow on the cheekbone that was hard enough to fell her to her knees. She felt the skin tear as she put out her hands to break the fall to the hard pavement. Another blow on her shoulder sent her temple against the concrete, and for an instant there was a black buzzing in her head.

She screamed, loudly, her cry echoing around the empty street and sensed rather than saw the next blow aimed at her mouth. She rolled sideways jarring herself against a thick-set leg, and shoved hard against it, her knuckles grinding into a hard shin. There was a harsh curse above her and she screamed again as she felt big, meaty hands grab the neck of her sweatshirt and twist violently. She could smell foul, beery breath and struck out blindly at the source, every horror story about assault and rape that she had ever read crowding sickly into her terrified mind.

There was another muffled grunt from her assailant

and then Ria felt a burning pain in her ribs. She screamed again as he kicked and kicked, and tried to bite viciously at the sour-smelling hand that pressed suffocatingly over her mouth. My God, was he trying to kill her? He was swearing at her as he bent over her, foul-mouthed promises of what he was going to do with her as he began to drag her sobbing, squirming body towards a hedged right-of-way.

Ria had never felt so frightened or helpless in her life. He was so big, so strong . . . She thrashed futilely in his agonising grip. Gathering all her strength she twisted her head away from the grinding hand on her mouth and gave one, last, choking cry. Unbelievably there came a blessed voice:

'Hey, What's going on out there?' It came from across the street. A man's voice, young and challenging. 'You over there, what are you doing?'

She was free. Tears streaming down her face, Ria lay painfully on her side as she heard the heavy, running stride of her attacker retreating.

'Are you all right? I heard you scream. What happened? Are you OK?' The young man in jeans and bare feet helped Ria limp across to his house, where he rang Paul and then the police.

There followed a slow, confused and painful hour when Ria gave her impossibly vague description of her attacker to the police and was examined by a doctor whom Paul had brought with him. There were no bones broken, but several painful scrapes and heavy bruising of her ribs and side. He put two stitches in her scalp where the concrete had made a small, deep cut and informed her cheerfully that she would probably have a black eye.

The police were doubtful, given the time lapse and her vague description, that they would find the man, and gave Ria the impression that the whole thing was her fault for being out on the streets alone at night.

Paul fussed and clucked and sent her to bed with a hot, milky drink, and surprisingly Ria slept well. She awoke next morning bruised and achy but determined, after a brief look in the mirror, to go to work. The bruise on her cheekbone could be covered by make-up and the slight discoloration of her eye would be hidden behind her glasses.

'Why don't you take the day off? Nobody would blame you for being a bit shaky the day after an assault. Stay home, Ria, and let me look after you.'

'I'm damned if I'll let that animal control anything I do,' said Ria, taking an aspirin with her coffee. It seemed to be a matter of honour that she should act completely normally, though she knew it would be a few evenings before she would go jogging again and she would make sure she went before dinner, when it was still light.

'I thought you said it was a man who jumped out on you, Mummy,' said Jamie, ever one for details.

'It was a man. I meant that he was acting like an animal,' Ria said.

'You should have had a gun, then you could have shot him,' said Michel. 'Pow!'

'Aaargh!' Jamie emitted a realistic dying gurgle. 'Or a knife strapped to your leg. You could have thrown it at him.' He threw an imaginary knife and this time it was Michel who squirmed and groaned.

'My bloodthirsty sons,' Ria said ruefully. 'I suppose I have television to thank for this.'

'It's not real blood on TV,' Michel informed her. 'It's only tomato sauce.'

'They get up afterwards. And then they go and have their lunch and if they have a pie they wipe it on the sauce,' his brother explained.

Ria set off with a grin, leaving Paul in the midst of a lecture about the difference between real and imaginary violence, trying to convince the two warriors that violence was not the answer to violence.

Ria got through the morning quite well, though the aspirin's effectiveness wore off by lunchtime and her

whole body seemed to merge into one long ache.
When J.E. left for lunch she sat limply down at her
desk, glad that he had spent most of the morning
absorbed in reading reports and leaving her more or
less to her own devices. He had hardly even looked at
her, and certainly hadn't had the time to study her in
the speculative way he had adopted of late. If he had
he surely would have noticed the stiffness evident in
her movements, and the scuff-mark on her cheek that
had begun to stand out darkly against her increasingly
pale complexion.

After half-heartedly eating a couple of sawdust
sandwiches and half an apple, Ria dragged herself to
her feet, intending to take another painkiller, when
Gerry walked in.

'J.E. back from lunch yet? Hey . . . you look terrible!'

'Thank you for those few kind words. No, he is
not.'

'Aren't you feeling well? Can I get you something to
take?'

Feeling too shaky to prevaricate, Ria told him. Gerry
had a few choice words to say about muggers and told
her to sit down while he went and fetched some water
for her pills.

'I thought I told you to sit down,' he said when he
came back, watching her swallow the two tablets.

'To tell the truth I think I've got some bruises there,
too,' she admitted tiredly, realising that reaction was
finally setting in, making her feel weak and weepy. She
should have stayed home instead of donning her stiff
upper lip. It made her feel sick to think of what had so
nearly happened twelve hours ago.

'Silly girl.' Gerry showed an affectionate concern that
was new to the usually indomitable Ria, taking gentle
hold of her hands. 'And I suppose you haven't told the
chief?'

'Told me what?' J.E. stood in the doorway, frowning
darkly at their clasped hands. Quickly Ria wrenched
hers free, managing to look a picture of guilt in the

process. J.E.'s frown intensified. 'Told me what?' he repeated.

Gerry opened his mouth, but Ria beat him to it. 'I'll tell him, Gerry.' She could see he was going to lay it on with a trowel. 'I'll be OK now, Gerry, thanks for caring.'

For a moment she thought he was going to insist on staying, but he contented himself with passing J.E. with: 'I hope you're going to send her home, she's nearly out on her feet.'

'He's exaggerating,' Ria insisted weakly after he had gone, and J.E. moved closer, seeing her pallor for the first time.

'What's he exaggerating? Are you ill? Why in God's name didn't you say something? There was no need to go running to Gerry about it.'

'I didn't go running. He came in and noticed I wasn't feeling well,' Ria defended herself. What a selfish beast he was, snapping at her just because he might be without his secretary for the afternoon!

'Hence the hand-holding. I see . . .' Goodness, surely he didn't imagine that she and Gerry . . .? 'What in the hell——?' The cold blue eyes had zeroed in on her cheek. He bent closer, his annoyance disappearing. 'What happened to your face? Your eye, too, by the looks of it.'

'I bumped it,' said Ria, tired of explaining the story to inquisitive males—the police, Paul, the twins, Gerry . . .

'A hell of a bump! How did you——?' He was cut off by her gasp of pain as he grasped her side to turn her more fully into the light. 'Ria?' Suspicion hardened his tone. 'Did you bump your side, too?' he asked sceptically.

Ria leaned against her desk as a wave of pain flowed over her, feeling the tears sting her eyes. She blinked them back, hating to cry in front of this man.

'Ria.' He moved his hands to her shoulders with amazing gentleness, his voice softening as he realised she was in real pain. 'I think you'd better tell me. Did someone do this to you? Who was it? Were you out with someone last night?'

Ria lifted her aching head to glare at him. 'Do I look like the kind of woman who dates muggers?'

'Muggers! You were attacked? When?' he fired at her, his jaw tightening as a stormy light entered his eyes.

'Last night.' Ria shrugged under the heavy, yet strangly comforting hands. 'While I was out jogging.'

'Alone?' There was censure in every line of his face. He reminded Ria of the policemen last night. She exploded with weary frustration.

'Yes, alone! It is allowed isn't it—in our free society? Women are permitted to go out on their own? Or are we supposed to sit at home in purdah because some men can't control their own greedy, lustful impulses? I suppose next you'll be saying that I was to blame. That a thick, baggy grey tracksuit is an incitement to rape?'

His olive skin paled visibly. 'My God, were you raped?' His eyes flickered down to her breasts, rounded beneath the plain white blouse, his hands sliding down her arms, bare beneath the short sleeves and looking quite delicate in his strong hands. When he reached her wrists he automatically turned them over and swore when he saw the grazed palms. 'Ria, he didn't——?'

'No, no,' Ria rushed in, knowing he wouldn't have paused delicately but ploughed straight into the nitty-gritty. He had an obsession with facts, with details, and if she had been raped he probably would have made her tell him everything. Her mouth went dry even thinking about it. 'I fought him, and someone heard me screaming and came out of a house. He ran off.'

'Did you call the police?' He raised her palms, inspecting them minutely, the lines prominent between his dark brows. 'Have you seen a doctor?'

'Of course I have, I'm not stupid.'

He ignored her sullen snap. 'Gerry's right, you should be at home.' Gently he replaced her hands at her sides, then lifted a finger to trace the slight bump on her cheekbone. 'Did he hit you in the face?'

She nodded. 'And I fell. He kicked me a few times, but his aim wasn't so good. I think he was drunk.'

'That's no excuse!' he said fiercely, as if she was defending her attacker. 'I'd like to get my hands on that bastard. What do the police say?'

'I didn't get a good enough look at him. Like you, they seemed to think I shouldn't have been out there jogging anyway.'

'You shouldn't,' he repeated firmly, again touching her cheek, noticing for the first time that under the make-up his sleek Miss Duncan had freckles. Though nothing had changed about her physically—except for the scrapes and bruises—she suddenly seemed smaller and less capable. There were traces of fear in the usually well-screened eyes, a new awareness of vulnerability that was oddly attractive. She really was quite small and delicately built, he realised. It was her cool aplomb that made her seem larger, more formidable. Right now she looked in need of a man's strength and understanding ... no wonder Gerry had held her hands and worn that protective look. James was tempted to do the same himself. He smiled at the way she stiffened at his words. Oh yes, she was a fighter ... thank God, she would never give in easily ... to an attacker or a lover.

Now what had made him think that? But she also needed to be made aware of the dangers that her usual self-confidence could, and obviously had, led her into.

'Of course you have a perfect legal right to freedom of movement, no one is disputing that. Only a moron would think that some of these drunken and sick minds require encouragement to indulge their twisted fantasies. But you have to face reality. It *should* be safe for women to walk the streets at night, but it's not. It *should* be safe for a woman to accept a lift home from a party from a strange man, but it's not. It you're going to do that sort of thing, you have to be prepared. Have you taken any self-defence courses?'

'I will now,' Ria said fervently, meaning it. She wasn't going to stop jogging, but she didn't want to be haunted by the knowledge of how helpless she was when confronted by male aggression.

'Good.' He smiled approvingly. 'Did you have someone to stay with you last night ... and tonight?' He didn't like to think of her alone, afraid.

'Yes.' Some of her aches were absorbed by rueful amusement. He was acting more like a father than a boss. 'Please don't fuss—people get attacked all the time, you know.'

'Not *my* people,' he said arrogantly, more the J.E. she knew.

'What should I do, wear a sign saying "Property of James Everett"?'

'If it'll keep the muggers away.' He grinned suddenly. J.E. never grinned. 'Perhaps I should get some T-shirts printed.'

'I don't think Mr Wallford would feel the expense justified,' she said, trying to stop the spread of a warm lethargy at his teasing.

'Mr Wallford is already aware that you're worth your weight in gold,' he remarked suavely. 'He wouldn't want to lose you either. Now, if I have to drive you home myself, you're going. Be a good girl and do as you're told for once, mmm?'

That was the second time in quarter of an hour she had been called a girl. 'I'm older than you are,' she asserted herself. 'I'm hardly a *girl* any more.'

'My apologies, ma'am,' he said, surprised. He had always thought of her as ageless. Certainly at the moment with her milky pale skin and big eyes blinking owlishly at him from behind her glasses, she didn't look over thirty. 'How old are you?'

'I'm th——' Ria's mind was travelling fuzzily, several seconds behind her mouth. She was too sore and too tired to try to figure out how old she was supposed to be. 'Oh, no, you don't get me that way, Mr Everett.' She shook her finger at him chidingly.

Her coyness was so out of character that James was taken aback. Firmly he steered her out to the bank of lifts and pressed the button.

'Here, here's some money.' He took her hand and pushed a note into it. 'There's a taxi rank downstairs. I want you to take one and call me in the morning to tell me how you feel.'

'Don't you mean take an asprin? A taxi would stick in my throat,' returned Ria, with what sounded to her buzzing ears a brilliant wit. Her headache was by now almost blinding her, but she clung desperately to a semblance of control.

'Very funny, Ria.' James' mouth curved with amused tolerance. His quiet office paragon had suddenly turned into an argumentative little soul. He wondered whether it was an aberration produced by the blow on her head or whether the pills and pain were giving him a glimpse of the real Ria Duncan for once. Whichever it was, he knew she would regret it tomorrow and the next time he saw her he would have his cool paragon back. The lift doors opened and he shepherded her in. 'Home, and straight to bed,' he ordered, grinning as the closing doors eclipsed her wrinkled brow. She had been trying to think of another smart reply. He went back to his office in a good mood and was even kind to the temporary secretary seconded from the typing pool.

Ria rode down in the lift wondering why he had been so nice. James Everett nice was a contradiction in terms. James Everett likeable was *dangerous*!

CHAPTER FIVE

RIA's cool and crisp greeting the next morning did not elicit the usual disinterested reply. Instead of immediately launching into the schedule for the day, J.E. leaned back in his chair, spreading his hands on his desk and studying her starchy appearance.

'So . . . Richard's himself again.' He grinned.

'Ria is *her*self again,' she corrected firmly, her mouth pinching in at the corners.

'If you're Ria, who was that feisty lady who was in here yesterday?'

'I have no idea,' she said coldly. This was even worse than she had feared. He was deliberately stepping outside that safe, conventional role that he had inhabited for so long. He was enjoying teasing her and she was aghast that a tiny part of her wanted to respond.

'Pity. I thought she was rather cute.'

Cute? Ria was outraged. What thirty-year-old woman wanted to be called cute? She swallowed a crackling reply and put on her best, blandest, ignore-his-tantrum face. 'Do you want to start the letters now? You have an appointment in twelve minutes——'

'How's the head? That cheek still looks tender. Did you see the doctor again?'

The switch from mockery to concern took her so much by surprise that she inadvertently admitted that her face was feeling rather stiff.

Ten minutes later she was in the company doctor's office being given a thorough check-up. When she returned to her desk she found a sheet of paper covered with J.E.'s compact italics. It was a list of all the self-defence courses currently available in the city. Ria frowned at it, wondering what he was trying to do. Was he attempting to make her feel some kind of pyschological obligation to him with all this interest in her personal welfare? A shiver went down her spine. Or did he have some deeper, darker motive?

For the next few days she was very careful to preserve a distance between herself and her boss. She congratulated herself that she succeeded, in spite of his non-cooperation and in spite of the mounting pressures from all sides. Louis was driving her mad with his obstinate telephone calls and Tony was firmly resisting her gentle discouragements. If she wasn't tied up with calls from one or the other at home she was breaking up the twins' wrestling matches. They seemed to be going through a particularly rowdy phase and in desperation Ria signed them both up with a soccer team, hoping that the organised chaos of twenty-two six-years-olds chasing a single ball would draw off some of their energy. Life, which only a month ago had been peaceful to the point of boredom was swinging to the opposite extreme. Now Ria felt that she was poised precariously on a high wire, juggling a handful of problems with no safety net.

Her balancing act couldn't last. A week after the attack a crisis arose that for the first time entailed Ria staying at the office after hours. It never even occurred to her to quibble, for lives were at stake.

The first inkling of trouble was a call from the BBC in London. Could James Everett confirm that he had a film crew shooting a documentary for a major charity in drought-stricken areas of Africa? Yes, he could. Could he also confirm that his crew was overdue at their next destination, in an area where there had been intensive troop activities over the last few days? He could not. Had he heard reports that rebels had been taking hostages amongst the civilian charity workers?

Grimly J.E. had terminated the call. The next few hours were long and frustrating ones. The crew were indeed overdue at a feeding station they were supposed to be visiting, but there had been no undue concern at

Everett Films because the team of four was travelling by truck, and was often out of contact for days at a time.

'You'd better start showing some concern now,' J.E. tautly informed the executive producer. 'Find out from your liaison people over there whether they have any information about the rebels taking hostages, use any channel you can.'

With ruthless persistence J.E. tapped his own Government sources, but the bureaucratic machinery was slow to engage and when results did begin to come in they were slim indeed. The African government in question had clamped down on the outflow of information and, with no diplomatic mission in the country, New Zealand couldn't press directly for action. Everything had to be channelled through the British.

Ria's respect for J.E.'s coolness under pressure increased as she watched him rip through the red tape and seek answers to questions that no one seemed able to handle. He showed quite remarkable patience, but by the time five o'clock rolled round enforced inaction was beginning to take its toll. He was like a tightly coiled spring, tensed to explode.

Ria quietly obeyed his staccato instructions, deftly handling the ordinary business of the day herself so that J.E. could concentrate on chasing a series of elusive leads. Six o'clock came and went and Gerry was sent to visit personally the families of the missing director, cameraman, sound operator and production assistant, and assure them that the company was doing all it could to track down their employees. During a lull Ria called Paul and told him not to expect her until late. Though J.E. had, at some stage, vaguely told Ria to go home, she had calmly ignored him. He needed someone there to express his frustration to, someone to share the relief—or the grief—if and when it came. He knew the cameraman personally, a man he had worked with when he had first started in advertising, and Ria knew that, although he didn't share it with her, his concern for the missing men was deeply personal as well as practical. Therefore she excused the few times he lashed out at her. He needed the safety value.

'I'm not hungry,' he said tersely, when she suggested ringing down a take-out order to the restaurant next door. 'Get something for yourself it you must. Carmichael? Any news?'

Ria waited until he had finished another fruitless call before she said gently, 'You should have something. You haven't eaten all day.'

'I told you I'm not hungry,' he snarled. 'I thought I told you to go home hours ago. You're not going to get overtime for this, you know.'

Ria turned on her heel and walked out. Twenty minutes later she carried in a covered tray and placed it on the coffee table.

'I thought you'd gone home,' he said gruffly, frowning at her, but she thought she saw a flicker of relief in his tense blue eyes.

'I'm far too used to your bite to be frightened by your bark,' she responded coolly, to counteract a rush of almost maternal sympathy for him. She was suddenly aware of the darkened sky outside the windows . . . the fact that they were almost alone in the building. She pushed the thought away. James Everett was tired, worried. It wouldn't hurt to give him some sympathetic company. She owed him *that* much.

'What's that?' He pointed to the tray.

'Chicken casserole and saffron rice.' She removed the cover. 'For me,' she said as he opened his mouth. 'Although there's enough for two if you change your mind.'

'I'll bet there is,' he said drily, aware of her technique, and of its probable success. Already the tantalising aroma was making his nostrils twitch, the hard knot in his belly slackening slightly as a healthy hunger eased some of his tension. It returned in full force as the green telephone at his elbow rang, shattering the quiet room with its raucous demand.

Ria watched as he reached reluctantly for the receiver, fatigue in every line of the body.

'Yes?'

There was a long, long silence as he listened. His face was rock-hard with concentration and Ria hardly dared breathe. Was this the call they had dreaded?

When he finally hung up she was almost screaming from the tension.

'Well?'

He got up, arching his back and rubbing his neck, pressing deeply into the aching muscle. 'There *are* hostages, five of them. But they're not our people ... they're medical staff from one of the clinics.' Ria expelled her breath, shuddering her relief. 'We still don't actually know where our film crew is, but as far as we know they're still alive. A Reuters correspondent spoke to them yesterday and got a message out somehow—garbled at first, that's how the BBC got fouled up. Apparently the army isn't allowing anyone in or out of the area yet, so it could be days before we know anything for certain. Meantime Foreign Affairs are pushing for some sort of official acknowledgement of their safety.'

'So what happens now?'

'We wait. Again.' Her grimace earned a vestige of a smile. 'But I don't think we'll hear anything more tonight. Let's eat, I'm famished.'

Ria was surprised at her own appetite, unaffected by J.E.'s closeness. She was at ease with him for the first time in weeks and it felt good. Even when he fetched a bottle of dry Californian red wine from his small bar she didn't demur. She realised that the day had also taken its toll of her. If J.E. had left well enough alone she might even have enjoyed the quiet sharing of a meal, but of course, once his physical appetite was satisfied he sought to amuse himself.

'Do I really bite?' he asked, sinking back into the comfort of the tweed couch where they sat, idly twisting his glass of wine in long fingers.

'Frequently,' Ria replied briefly, straightening her back so that she sat warily on the edge of her seat. She mistrusted the gleam in his blue eyes, studying her at leisure.

'Then why don't you bite back?'

'I'd probably break my teeth on your hide.'

'You might be surprised how tender my hide is . . . in places.'

He sipped his wine and rolled the full-bodied warmth around his mouth while he watched her absorb that one and calculate whether it was safe to answer.

'I prefer to let sleeping dogs lie. They can be too unpredictable if you poke them.' She began to stack the plates and cutlery on the tray.

'Leave those, for God's sake.' He picked up her half-empty glass and thrust it at her. 'Drink your wine. You can do all that later.'

Ria finished her drink quickly, and then was sorry. It gave her something to do with her hands.

'Here.' To her dismay he leaned over and poured some of his wine into her glass, and when she stared at it he guided her glass to her lips and held it there, tilting it so that the wine slid down her throat. He watched the rippling movement of her throat above the high-buttoned cream blouse. 'Sip it slowly this time, I don't want to have to carry you home. You obviously haven't mastered the fine art of relaxing.'

'You're a fine one to talk,' Ria pointed out. 'At least I relax at home, you take your office with you.'

'I'm relaxed now,' he said, lounging against the tweed cushions, and Ria had to agree. His shirt sleeves were rolled up past muscular forearms coated in dark hair, his collar was open to his breastbone, revealing more thick curls. His hair was tousled and the dark shadow on his angular jaw made him a picture of unkempt virility.

'Do you think we'll get any more news in the morning? Should I come in early?' she asked, uneasy at the lilt in his voice.

He smiled lazily. 'Don't change the subject.'

'I wasn't, I was just——'

'Of course you were, you do it all the time ... but usually you're a bit more subtle about it, so that it's not until afterwards that I remember I'm supposed to be tearing someone limb from limb. There are people in this building who owe their jobs to your ability to soothe the savage beast, or at least distract him long enough to whip away the bone.'

'If this is another attempt to make me feel that I'm wasting my talent just being a secretary——'

'Not at all. I've changed my mind about that,' he declared, resting his head against the tweed and closing his eyes. 'I've decided that I prefer you as my secretary.'

'You have?' Ria was highly suspicious.

'Mmmm. I have a feeling that if I give you a taste of the freedom power can give you there'd be no stopping you. In a year I'd be fighting you for *my* job.'

'I wish you'd be serious,' she snapped, annoyed by the faint smile curling his lips, giving his whole face a rakish tilt.

'Why? What does it matter what my reason is? I've finally accepted that you're stubborner than I am. Just accept it.' He turned his head and opened his eyes, catching her looking at his mouth. 'It would do you good to be a little less serious. Or does it take a whack on the head for you to succumb to the occasional smile? Look at you, stiff as a board and about as comfortable. Why are you so afraid to relax with me? It's not forbidden, is it? Do you belong to some secret sect that demands a stiff upper lip at all times?'

'Don't be silly. I just don't think that we ought to ... that you and I ... that we ...' She floundered deeper and deeper, beginning a slow blush at his deep laugh. He moved his weight on to his hip, curving his body to face hers. There were inches of tweed between them, but Ria felt as if he had moved on top of her.

'Why, Miss Duncan, what can you be suggesting?' he mocked languidly, finishing his wine and leaning forward to put down his glass. His leg brushed deliberately against hers and her knee-jerk reaction was automatic.

He raised his eyebrows. 'Are you implying that you find something indecent about the idea of us relaxing together? It depends, of course, where we relax, but I can't see the harm in the office couch. For one thing it's too short for what you obviously have in mind, though it does raise some unexpected possibilities.'

Ria's face glowed almost as red as her hair and he added, his voice stifled with laughter, 'Did you know that your freckles stand out when you're angry?'

She was passionately grateful for the phone call that interrupted his teasing. Unfortunately it was for her, and the only person she could think of who would ring her at the office was Paul.

'I'll take it in my office,' she said, jumping to her feet.

'Take it here,' he ordered. 'And make it short, I want to keep the lines open just in case.' His eyes narrowed when she hesitated. 'Or shall I speak to *him* for you?'

Paul, it must be. She hoped that one of the boys wasn't ill. Snatching the receiver she said warily, 'Hello?'

'Ria?'

She jerked upright, staring in horror at James, who made no move to give her any privacy.

'Louis!' She had completely forgotten that he was supposed to visit her this evening. No, perhaps forgotten was the wrong word. She had been dreading facing him again and her mind had welcomed the chance to push the confrontation into the background.

'Ria, surely this problem Paul told me about isn't going to keep you any longer? There can't be anything that *you* can do. I've been waiting here for you for hours.'

'I'm sorry.' Conscious of the intent interest with which J.E. was registering her distress Ria half-turned away and lowered her voice. 'I'm sorry, Louis, I really am, but I really can't get away yet. We'll just have to make it another time.'

'Another time?' Louis's cultured voice was sharply aggrieved. 'Ria, you know very well that the only reason I flew in was to talk to you. I have an important meeting in Sydney tomorrow, then I'm going on to Japan. Surely our future has precedence over this problem of Everett's? After all, there's nothing that you can actually do tonight, is there?'

'We haven't *got* a future, Louis,' she hissed. 'We've been through all this before, and there is nothing more to talk about.'

'How can you say such a thing? Of course we must talk. Now you've had time to think it ov——'

'Louis!' Ria screeched, biting off her hasty words as she threw a furtive glance at her audience. He looked fascinated. 'Louis, I am tired of being treated like a child. I made up my mind weeks ago, I can't help it if you won't accept my decision.' She was smugly pleased to see James Everett's frown of puzzlement as she switched into rapid French. She smiled sweetly at his totally blank expression as she proceeded to use brutality where reason had failed. 'I am not going to marry you, I never will. But perhaps we could come to some other arrangement.'

'Arrangement? Ria, what are you talking about?' Louis followed her lead, swapping languages without question.

'Why bother with marriage? It's so boring. And it means all sorts of upheavals. Why don't I just become your mistress? Whenever you come to New Zealand I can come and stay with you at your hotel. All the fun of the party with none of the hangovers. Isn't that a marvellous idea?'

There was dead silence at the other end of the phone, but Ria could hear stentorian breathing. Poor Louis, this time she hoped she had shocked him beyond recall.

'That is a very poor joke, Ria,' he said finally, his voice creaking with disapproval. 'A dishonour to René. A dishonour to Paul. A dishonour to your children.

And an insult to me.'

How dare he mention René, who had loved her with exuberant passion, in the same breath as himself ... a stolid, practical hypocrite! 'Well, I'm sorry you feel that way, Louis, but that's my final offer,' she said icily, 'take it or leave it.'

'I'm very disappointed in you, Ria——'

'How the hell would you know, you've never tried me!' she yelled at him crudely and smashed the telephone receiver back into its cradle. Pompous idiot! She was furious at herself for feeling guilty at her treatment of him. What else could she have done? She had visions of years of being pursued relentlessly by Louis and his dour proposals.

'Finished?'

'Yes.' She had forgotten all about him in that final, heated exchange. She pictured Louis taking his offended leave of her father-in-law. At least his mother would be pleased, now she was free to line him up with one of the aristos she had had in mind for him all along.

'Don't you know that it's very rude to speak a foreign language in front of people who don't understand it?' Hands on lean hips, he looked like a typically arrogant male.

'It's also rude to try and eavesdrop on other people's private conversations,' she replied sharply, her nervous awareness of him temporarily abolished by her anger.

'If you choose to conduct your sex-life in my office, over my telephone, you can hardly accuse me of eavesdropping.'

Ria's jaw dropped. His accent was grating but his words, and by implication his understanding, were quite fluent.

'You beast! How dare you!' She went red, then white with fury.

'How I dare speak French? What a snob you are, Ria. Just because I dropped out of school at fourteen doesn't mean I have to stay ignorant for the rest of my life. I can speak a bit of Japanese, too.'

'Why didn't you say something, you ... you ...! Her rage almost choked her. Frantically she tried to recall what she had said to Louis. What she had revealed.

'I was riveted,' he said in a slow silky voice that made her heart sink, 'not only by what you were trying to hide, but by the way you chose to hide it. You were trying to put both of us in our places at once, but you bit off more than you could chew. I won't be put, Ria, except where I choose to be put ... unlike that poor sod on the other end of the line.'

Ria took a step towards him and then stopped, her eyes blazing green fire. Red tendrils of hair had begun to drift out of her neat top-knot.

'There is nothing *poor* about Louis, I can assure you. Any woman who married him would have to be an angel of——' She could have bitten off her tongue for using the word when she saw his eyes widen in sudden comprehension. His hand moved up, even as she reared back, and flipped the glasses off her nose. She made a grab and missed. He stepped back, the glasses in his hand, and ran his eyes over her face.

'My God,' he said through his teeth, 'no wonder I thought there was something about you, something different I couldn't put my finger on, and it was staring me in the face all the time. You're the red-head from the restaurant. I remember your eyes ...' His own dropped lower, '... among other things, of course.'

Ria found her voice, an appalling little thing that wavered alarmingly. 'Mr Everett——'

He smiled unpleasantly. 'Was *that* poor Louis you abandoned for my nephew? No wonder he's anxious to curtail your freedom.'

Ria closed her eyes briefly. Oh, no, now he was going to put two and two together and realise that she was Tony's mystery Frenchwoman. But James Everett was on an entirely different tack.

'But you must have known who *I* was, why didn't you say something?' Her eyes flew open again, dismayed even more by what she saw on his face. It had a smouldering intensity that made her wish he *had* realised the truth. She would far rather handle his anger than this stomach-wrenching type of sensual amusement. 'Were you too embarrassed? Or perhaps you were curious to know what I tasted like, and felt it was safe there in the anonymous darkness. Is that what it was, Ria?'

'Mr Everett, you're wrong——' Ria shook her head, feeling that anything was better than letting him think that she had deliberately led him on.

'Really? Well, there's a simple way of finding out.'

'W . . . what do you mean?' she stuttered, not understanding him.

'I mean, a woman's kisses are like her fingerprints . . . they have certain individual characteristics. It should be easy to prove, or disprove, that you were the woman in the restaurant.'

'No, no——' Ria backed away, putting up her hands, trying to tell him that she wasn't trying to deny, only explain. 'Mr Everett, I——'

He caught her easily by the elbows and jerked her forward. 'Too late for that, Ria, you're not going to humour me out of this one. I'm looking forward to it too much.' He lowered his mouth, taking his time.

'It was me, of course it was me!' Ria cried in panic, trying to turn her head and struggle at the same time. 'You don't have to——' Her mouth was muffled by his, the harshness of his beard rasping over her chin as he wedged her head against his shoulder and held her tightly, blissfully trapped while he explored her rashly parted lips.

His mouth was incredibily warm and gentle and incredibly familiar. Ria felt her body weaken, her struggles die as he played with her, mouth brushing, opening and closing over hers, taking small, savoury bites of her soft lips, slipping his tongue into her silky moistness while his powerful arms slid around her waist and wrapped her against his lean hardness.

Ria's head swam as she was reacquainted with the

sweet-sharp pleasure she had experienced once before in his arms, and tried so unsuccessfully to forget. The tantalising movements of his lips made her long for more. A soft sound murmured up in her throat as his hands slid up between her shoulder blades, rubbing firmly, pressing her breasts to his warm chest. The hard edge of his hipbone wedged itself into her soft abdomen and his thighs moved restlessly against hers. Summoning a vestige of common sense Ria tried to stiffen her trembling limbs, to dampen down the slow fires that the lanquid thrusts of his tongue were igniting, but they were too scattered and fierily sweet.

He freed her mouth at last so that he could take nibbling bites of softly curving jaw. 'Mr Everett . . . sir . . . *James*!' she wailed gaspingly, but he only laughed.

'The prosecution rests,' he murmured huskily into her skin. With one hand splayed on her upper back he used the other to tilt her face back and kiss her again, harder, less teasingly. The soft pad of his thumb caressed her tender earlobe, stroking over the pearl stud and fondling the downy flesh. Ria had never been aware of her ears as erogenous zones before, but James was manipulating the tiny gold post that threaded through her lobe with a delicate and knowing skill that sent delicious tingles streaking out over her body.

Ria shivered with dangerous delight. She could feel her breasts swelling tightly against the lace of her bra and experienced an aching desire for his touch. As if he sensed her innermost needs, his hands shifted to grip her above the waist, his thumbs digging into the sides of her swollen breasts. But instead of fondling her, he anchored her firmly and began to move his torso, twisting it slowly from side to side so that the hard wall of muscle that was his chest rubbed teasingly back and forth, intensifying her arousal. It was as though he was massaging her entire body with his. Ria had never felt such an excruciatingly sensuous frustration, the urge to bite and kick and fight and *make* him take her.

Suddenly she was free and they were both staring at

each other, breathing hard, six inches between them that radiated with crackling energy, a force-field alive with sexual tension. His nostrils flared as he looked at her love-bitten mouth and his smile was a mixture of bemusement and arousal.

'I might have forgotten what you looked like, but I sure as hell didn't forget that angel mouth. No more lies, Ria.'

'I wasn't——' She coughed to clear her throat, and took a breath to try and rid herself of the taste and scent of him. Her voice was as husky as his. 'I never intended to deny it. You didn't need to kiss me.'

'How do you know what I need?' he asked, blue eyes swimming with a lazy sensuality. How it changed him from the James Everett she thought she knew! Ria resisted the tug of attraction and squared her shoulders sensibly.'

'May I have my glasses back, please?' she asked as calmly as she could, holding out a hand then snatching it back as she saw how much she was shaking.

'Why? Can't you see me properly? Is that your excuse for the other night? Are you long or short-sighted?'

To her horror he rubbed the lenses briefly against his silk shirt and held them up to the light. The smile froze on his face and he lowered them slowly, turning, his expression chilling.

'What in the hell are you playing at?'

Ria smoothed her hands down the side of her skirt. It had been a long, long day and she had the ghastly feeling it was going to turn out to be one of the worst of her life. Without her glasses she felt strangely naked. René had always told her what expressive eyes she had. Right now she fervently hoped that it had only been loving flattery. Then she thought, what the hell, my ideal job is down the tubes anyway! She would never be able to work for James Everett after this.

'You made the rules,' she said, looking him straight in the eye. His head went up and back, the shadowed jaw clenching.

'*I* made them?' There was anger as well as bafflement in the terse demand. He was tapping her spectacles against the back of his hand as if he would like to smash them. '*I* made you wear glasses you don't need? I made you screw your hair up like a Chinaman? No wonder I didn't recognise you ... Miss Prunes and Prism. Are you claiming *I* asked you to put on some incredible act? Who was it supposed to benefit?'

'No you didn't *ask*, but it was what you expected, wasn't it?' Ria flung at him, glad at once for it to be out in the open. She hadn't realised how much she had resented the double life she had been leading. She had thought that it suited her, but it didn't, it was like a strait-jacket and she was sick of it. 'Didn't you ever wonder—wonder *why* I was so perfect for this job?' She felt infuriated by his surprise. 'No, of course you didn't, you just arrogantly assumed that I must have been put on this earth for the sole purpose of filling your need for a secretary. Well, I was perfect because I *made* myself perfect.'

Defiantly she told him in explicit detail what she had overheard him say to Gerry in that coffee bar, enjoying the stunned expression on his face.

'You didn't want a woman, you wanted a ... a ... *thing*. And I wanted the money you were offering.'

'You went to such lengths merely to satisfy your mercenary instincts?' he jeered suspiciously, and Ria knew instantly what he was thinking.

'What other reason could there be?' she demanded contemptuously. 'You wouldn't have trusted any *normal* woman; she wouldn't have passed your "test"! Mr Irresistible ... so certain that every woman who walked into your office would be yours for the asking ... or rather, for the *not* asking.' She was furiously pleased to see a tinge of redness creep across his cheekbones above the concealing shadow on his jawline.

'I grant an attractive red-head might not have been my first choice,' he grated back. 'But why bother with the charade for so long? Once you'd established yourself why didn't you just tell me?'

'Oh, sure,' scoffed Ria heatedly. 'You probably would have thought it was all part of the plan. Worm my way into the job then devastate you by revealing my hidden beauty!'

He was icily annoyed by her sarcasm. 'I said attractive, not beautiful,' he said with chilly emphasis. 'As long as you were good at your job I wouldn't have cared what you looked like once you had proved yourself. I'm not *that* neurotic. Or that arrogant.' The last three words were faintly dry as he began to appreciate the ironic humour of the situation. Looking at Ria now he couldn't believe he had been so blind for so long.

'You say that *now*.' In her temper Ria missed the nuances in his tone. 'But how was I to know? You're always talking about how important honesty and loyalty are. For all I knew you would have fired me on the spot.'

'What makes you think I'm not going to do that now?' he countered silkily. 'Because I've kissed you a few times? I've kissed women before, and fired them.'

'I'm quite aware of how fickle and indiscriminate you are,' she snapped, angry with both herself and him. She *had* thought that he wouldn't fire her, not because of the kisses but because lately he had appeared to show her a new trust, the beginnings of a respect of her not only as a secretary, but as a person in her own right. She had been wary of it, afraid even, but also rather flattered. Who wouldn't be?

'Anyway, you can't fire me,' she drove herself on, 'because I quit!' The words ricocheted around the room at high velocity, regretted as soon as they were uttered.

He turned and walked away towards the window. With every step Ria felt herself go a little colder. She didn't want to lose her job. She liked it too much. In spite of the hard work, the tension, and the infuriating man staring out into the darkened city, she liked it. Of course, the money was the *main* reason she didn't want to lose her job, she told herself, unaware that she was holding her breath. But she couldn't force herself to utter a word of regret or defence. She wouldn't crawl to him. She had deceived him but not in any way that compromised his position of head of Everett Communications.

'You can't quit.' The implacable words bounced off the cool glass and reached Ria just as she thought she was going to pass out from lack of air.

'Why not?' she demanded and stiffened as he turned back to face her. He was smiling, a wry, knowing smile as he read the mixture of hope and defiance in her wavering gaze.

'Because I need you too much. We make too good a team to break up.' He came forward, his hands spread palm upwards in a self-deprecating gesture. It was Ria's turn to be suspicious. It was unlike J.E. to back down so suddenly and so completely. He was actually coaxing. 'Come, I've admitted that you had some justification for your actions, can't you admit that I had some, too? Until you came those damned women were driving me mad.'

He was inviting her to share his amusement in a way that melted Ria's resistance. She didn't want to resist anyway.

'I rather thought the boot was on the other foot,' she said with a tiny answering smile.

'That's why you have to stay.' He grinned, shedding the humble approach with triumphant ease at her green-eyed acquiescence. 'Think of it as a kind of preventive measure ... rescuing those of us less pragmatic than yourself from the horrors of mutual insanity.'

CHAPTER SIX

INSANITY. Later Ria wondered if she wasn't already suffering from it. Why else hadn't she grabbed the perfect opportunity to tell him the truth—the entire truth? Once his initial outburst was past he behaved as if he found the idea of her sustained fraud rather amusingly clever. Perhaps it was the novelty of being fooled at all that caught his fancy. She doubted that he would be as amused, and forgiving, a second time. The novelty would have worn off by then.

The trouble was that now he thought that he had unmasked her, he expected her behaviour to change accordingly. That evening, before he had let her go, he had returned her glasses with a jibe about her acquiring contact lenses.

'I . . . thought I might keep wearing these.' She weighed the frames in her hand. 'People might think it's odd if——'

'They'll think it odder still if they see me tearing them off you and stamping them to pieces,' he told her stubborn expression. 'Although I must admit there would be a certain piquancy in having the starchy, bespectacled Miss Duncan around . . . particularly since only I would know the delicious truth beneath the clothes. Yes, if you like you can go on wearing your disguise.'

She had glared at him. His mock agreement with its sexual undertones made it impossible, and he knew it. Her disguise hid nothing from him anymore, and by continuing with it she would only emphasise what she was trying to conceal. Damn him!

'You could drop a hint or two that you've discovered a new hairdresser as well as optician,' he said slyly. 'Not to mention the fountain of youth. You'll be the envy of the building!'

'It won't be a very miraculous transformation,' she said coolly. 'I'll still be older than you are.'

He sat down on his desk and inspected her. 'Incidentally, how old *are* you? With skin like that you could be a young girl.'

'I'm thirty,' she said, crossly flattered. 'As a matter of fact, it was my birthday that night at the restaurant.'

'I'm so glad I was there to help you celebrate,' he teased. 'Did poor Louis give you as exciting a gift as I did?'

'As it happens he had an engagement ring for me.'

'How disappointing for you; and you were hoping for his hotel key!'

'Very amusing.'

'Get to know me better I can be even more amusing,' he said complacently, the subtle shadings in his tone infinitely disturbing to Ria's nervous system.

'Mr Everett——'

'James, call me James.' He crossed one leg casually over the other, the fabric straining against his thigh. He clicked his tongue at her expression. 'Who's to know, Ria? You can be as officious as you damned well like in company, but what's the point when we're alone? Surely we've gone beyond all this "sir" stuff.'

That's what Ria was afraid of. 'Why do I get the feeling I'm being manipulated in some grand plan of yours?'

'The feeling's mutual, darling.' He grinned, the mobility highlighting his attractiveness and lessening the threat of that beaky nose. 'After all, yours was the grandest plan of all.'

'Are you going to throw that at me every time we——'

'Have a row?' he inserted wickedly, making it all sound very domestic. 'I won't if you won't—throw my lurid past at me, I mean. We start again, from scratch. Deal?'

The idea *sounded* all right, but Ria frowned. There was a catch in there somewhere if she could only have the time to figure it out.

'And from now on we'll be completely honest. No more disguises. So if you have any more insults or complaints or confession, let's hear them now.'

She hesitated, and was lost. She already felt horribly vulnerable, by opening up to him she would be inviting rejection . . . hurt. He was attracted to her quality of elusiveness and would no doubt be disappointed by the commonplace reality. She couldn't imagine James being keen on children. If he ever thought of settling down it would be with someone like Marie Steele—young, carefree, with no past to complicate things. And if they had children they would be expected to fit in with their parents' liftstyle rather than vice versa.

The more she thought about it, the more necessary it seemed to withhold the deepest, and most vulnerable, part of herself from the cynical gaze of James Everett— the seat of love, maternal, emotional, romantic, as separate from the purely physical senses which he had already invaded.

At least there had been one concrete gain from the night of crisis. Louis had finally got the message. He had sent her a stiff little note stating that perhaps, sometime in the future, they might be friends again. Ria doubted it. Pride and politeness had dictated the note but Louis would never follow it up.

Paul had been philosophical when she told him, so much so that she thought he was secretly relieved. As for Jamie and Michel, they took it calmly in their stride when she told them that their Uncle Louis might not be visiting any more.

'Does that mean he won't be sending me any more stamps?' asked Michel, an avid collector.

'I really don't know,' said Ria as she helped them into their pyjamas. 'But I can still get lots for you from work.'

'Isn't he going to be our father, then?'

Ria sat on the edge of Jamie's bed as he scrambled in. 'Did you want him to be your father?' She felt a surge of guilt. Was she being overly selfish? Had the boys become more attached to Louis than she had thought?

'It would have been OK, I guess,' said Jamie, a marked lack of enthusiasm on his face. 'I don't think he likes soccer very much.'

'I'd rather have our own dad,' said Michel in a small voice.

Ria reached out to squeeze the small brown hand resting on top of the blankets, 'I know, but I'm afraid that Daddy can't be with us.'

'Couldn't he come and visit?' The brown eyes showed a mixture of hurt puzzlement.

'Of course he can't, he's in Heaven,' said Jamie knowledgeably.

'Is he God?'

'Course he isn't. We've got photographs of Daddy, haven't we, Mummy? You can't take pictures of God,' Jamie insisted.

Ria could see that something else was troubling Michel. Less outgoing than his twin he was given to bottling things up. She shifted over to his bed and ruffled his hair. 'You know, sometimes I miss your Daddy dreadfully, but I know that he would want us to be happy, and not to worry about him being away from us. He loved you very much, even though you were only tiny babies when he knew you.'

'Steven in our class ...' Michel's plump lower lip trembled, '... Steven says that his Dad ran away because he hated his Mummy.'

'Oh, darling!' Ria bent over to hug her son tightly. 'Daddy didn't run away from us. He was very very badly hurt. You wouldn't have wanted Daddy to be always hurting, would you?' A vigorous shake of a black head. 'So God took him so that he would never hurt again. We can't see him or talk to him, or have him back but we can keep him in our hearts.'

'Are *you* going to die?'

Ria felt a sweet pain as she wondered how to answer. Should one be reassuring? Or should one tell the truth?

Sometimes she wished that her boys would never grow up, that they would always be innocent and trusting and safe in their childish belief in the world. But she knew that she couldn't protect them forever, that they needed to grow and explore in their own way. She could only love, and let them go when the time came. She had to be careful not to smother them. Ever since she had begun work, a large part of their young lives were lived separately from her. She worried about it acutely and had to restrain herself from being over-conscientious during their precious times together. That was one reason why she was so adamant that her work didn't encroach on her private life.

'All living things die eventually, but they give birth to new life . . . like I did to you. And I hope to be here for a very long, long time yet, to see you grow up and get married and have children of your own one day.'

That seemed to reassure him, but Jamie wasn't ready to snuggle down to sleep. He had thought of something else.

'Will we ever get another daddy? Steven's mother has new daddies all the time.'

The relationship was confused but Ria grasped the essentials. 'Well, I suppose it depends on whether I meet a man nice enough to marry,' she said carefully.

'Wasn't Uncle Louis nice enough?' Michel piped up innocently.

'Not quite,' Ria replied judiciously.

'Why don't you ask Steven's mummy, she knows lots of nice men.'

'I'm sure she does, thought Ria, remembering the gossip at the last P.T.A. meeting she had attended. 'Steven's mummy doesn't work. I don't have time to meet lots of men.'

'The Beast won't let her. She's his slave,' Jamie informed his brother.

'Jamie! Of course I'm not. Whatever gave you that idea?' Ria cried, horrified.

'That's what Uncle Louis said. He said Mr Everett was a slave-driver.'

'He didn't really mean it,' said Ria, guessing this was said on the night that she hadn't come home.

'Does that mean he doesn't really have big teeth, either?' asked Michel, his eyes beginning to droop.

'Why should he have big teeth?' Ria asked warily. She thought of all the times she had complained to Paul in the twins' hearing, all the throwaway lines they might have taken literally, and shuddered.

'To suck people's blood. You said people come out from his office with no blood in them.'

'Did I?' Ria said weakly, trying not to laugh. 'I think I said "bloodless", it just means that sometimes he frightens people a bit. Actually Mr Everett is a very—— ' She caught herself just in time. Nice, she was going to say and after her comments earlier about daddies she thought that would be fatal, '—very good employer. He offered me a promotion the other day.'

'What's a pr'motion?' asked Jamie, diverted.

'A more important job.'

'Are you going to be boss?' Michel yawned sleepily, his earlier fears put to rest, now just wanting to prolong the bedtime ritual.

'Girls can't be bosses,' scoffed Jamie.

'Mrs Carmel is boss of our school.'

'That's only of kids. Girls can't be bosses of men.'

'Girls can be anything they want,' Ria declared firmly, determined to nip male chauvinism in the bud. She stood up and smoothed both beds.

'Are you going to be boss then?' asked Jamie meekly.

'No, Mr Everett wanted me to be his assistant, but I said no.'

'Why?'

Ria compressed a smile. Jamie and James obviously thought alike . . . always questioning.

'Because it would mean that I couldn't spend as much time with you two. I might even have to miss your soccer games when you start playing on Saturdays.'

That clinched it. 'I'm glad you don't want to be more important,' mumbled Michel.

'Me too,' said Jamie. He whispered in her ear as she switched off the lamp and gave he and his teddy a kiss: 'I'm glad you're not going to marry Uncle Louis. He stepped on my toe.'

'Did he?' Ria whispered back. 'I hope he said sorry.'

'Yes, but he called me Michel.'

'That's not entirely his fault,' she said fairly. 'Most people can't tell you apart.'

'A real daddy would,' he protested indignantly.

'Yes, but they're special. I promise I won't marry anyone who can't tell you apart. How about that?' she teased.

'OK.' He was silent for a minute. 'If you can't find anyone, Michel and I will look.'

Ria went downstairs laughing, and shared with Paul the arresting prospect of having a husband selected for her on the basis of a six-year-old's definition of 'nice'.

'You could do worse, Chérie,' he grinned, taking the pipe from his mouth. 'At least you could be sure that he'd be a lot of fun.'

'Mmmm, a cross between Superman and Father Christmas.' She shuddered at the thought. 'I'm too old to look a fun marriage in the eye.'

'Perhaps you should have married Louis then,' Paul puffed cunningly.

'Mmmmm, there must be a middle course I could steer,' Ria said as she sat down to another quiet evening's sewing. In a month or so the weather would be getting cooler and the boys had long grown out of last winter's clothes. She was grateful that her mother, who had been a fine dressmaker, had passed on some of her skills, if not her flair.

The next morning she was glad of that peaceful evening. J.E. left for a stockholders' meeting at nine and she heard nothing from him until Gerry sought her out at half past eleven.

'He wants you to meet him there at noon.'

'Why?' Ria frowned, looking at the work piled up around her.

'It being the name of a restaurant, Ria,' Gerry said with laborious slowness, 'I would say that you're probably going to have lunch.'

'But my lunch hour isn't until one o'clock.'

'He must have forgotten.'

Ria met twinkling blue eyes, so much more easy to read than that other, enigmatic pair. Oh no, James hadn't forgotten. He was just making sure that she couldn't refuse. Twice in the last four days he had asked her to lunch with him and she had refused, saying he couldn't dictate her actions during her own time.

'Maybe it's a business lunch,' she said.

'Well, you can't very well not turn, up, can you, not when there's an off chance?'

'Why shouldn't I turn up?' Ria asked coolly.

Gerry flashed white teeth. 'Ria, this is the exec. assist. you're talking to. A blind, deaf and dumb man wouldn't have had much trouble picking up the vibrations around here lately.'

'Gerry . . .'

He held up his hands. 'Haven't said a word, Ria. And if you're worried about the rumour factory, forget it. It's been humming for weeks now, particularly since the sudden blooming in your looks. Haven't you noticed how much traffic up here has increased?'

'There's nothing going on, Gerry,' Ria said firmly.

'I know that, and you know that, but has anyone told the chief?'

Ria sailed into the restaurant in top gear, determined to set her boss straight on a few points. He had no right to use these tactics on her just because she had refused to become any further involved with him. It rather took the wind out of her sails to find out that he was late. She had to cool her heels for fifteen minutes at the table, angrily sipping a dry martini.

Part of the trouble was that she had refused his invitations too quickly, thereby giving him the impression that she *wanted* to accept but was too scared to. The other part of the trouble was that his impression would have been right. She was afraid that she might enjoy herself too much in his company. When he put himself out to be pleasant, as he had in the last few days, it was hard not to wonder how much *more* pleasant he might be, given the opportunity. Which he wouldn't be, Ria told herself severely, as she stiffened at the sight of his dark head being greeted by the waiter.

She watched him walk casually across the room, her stomach tightening at the twists and turns of his body as he skirted the tables, greeting several people in passing. He couldn't have chosen a more public venue to bring her.

'I could see your freckles all the way across the room,' he said as he slid down into the chair opposite and ordered a drink. 'I suppose you're mad at me.'

'Is this business?' she demanded stiffly, conscious of curious eyes around them, particularly female ones. The martini began to simmer in the pit of her stomach.

'I have some news about our camera crew,' he said, his smile replaced by a grave expression that made Ria feel terrible. She had been so certain that he had brought her here for some nefarious purpose that she felt a worm for having misjudged him.

'Your friend . . . is he all right?' she asked, her green eyes softening with sympathy as he leaned forward. She knew that their failure to discover the fate of the missing film crew had weighed heavily on his mind.

'They're all OK, they arrived in Kenya last night. I got a call at the meeting. They did have a breakdown, then they ran into some troops and went through some pretty tough questioning . . . but no physical stuff.'

Ria breathed a sigh of relief. 'Couldn't you have told me this at the office?'

'I want to celebrate with someone,' he said disarmingly. 'And since you shared the trauma I wanted you to share the relief.'

'Why here?' She swept the room, noting they were

still drawing some attention and, no doubt, some speculation. 'Why couldn't we have gone some-where——'

'Small, intimate?' His eyes mocked her. 'Why, Ria, I thought you'd feel safer in a public place. I thought if I brought you here you couldn't possibly suspect my motives.'

'And what are you motives?' she asked, knowing he had her well and truly tied up with her own objections.

'Entirely honourable!' He laid a hand across his heart. 'I merely want us to get to know each other a little better. Be comfortable with each other.'

'You're joking!' Ria couldn't be comfortable with him, not when he made her nerves jump the way he did, not when his presence was like sandpaper on the thin skin of her composure.

'So you feel it too,' he murmured softly, with no pretence now of innocence. Ria was aware that her exclamation had given away some vital information that up until now she had done her best to conceal. She fussed over the menu as the waiter came up, but she ordered the lightest, simplest, fastest thing she could find—an asparagus omlette. James followed suit with seafood crêpes and teased her when she refused wine.

'Afraid you'll lose you head over me?'

'There's no danger of that,' she said, lowering her lashes over the fib.

'Not even the least bit curious?'

'No.' She had been curious ever since that first kiss.

'Then why won't you look at me? You try not to, these days, now you haven't got those glass prisons to shelter behind. I suppose you're afraid of what I'll see.'

She lifted her eyes bravely and he smiled, tiny lines curving sensuously at the corners of his mouth.

'Lovely, lying eyes . . . like the sea, wide and deep and ever changing.'

'James——'

'I'm not about to jeopardise the good working relationship we have, Ria,' he asserted gently, 'I'm just asking you to let things develop naturally between us. Don't put up barriers all the time.'

'I thought you didn't like your secretaries chasing you,' she muttered, not having to ask what he meant by 'things'. He was talking about an affair, and apart from the practicalities of her situation preventing any such relationship, there was her certainty that it would be wrong. Not morally, but wrong for Ria Masson.

'But you're not. Quite the reverse.'

There. It was said, out loud. He wanted her. 'Maybe it's just a ploy,' she said desperately, 'playing hard to get.'

'For what purpose?'

'To trap you.' She smiled blindly at the waiter who delivered her meal, and began to eat mechanically.

'Trap me into what? An affair? Lead me to the stake!'

'Marriage,' she said, ignoring the glass of wine he had poured from the icy bottle. Surely the word would scare him off.

He laughed, and she could see that he was genuinely amused. There was a light-heartedness about him that was different. Was it the result of hearing about his friends? Or was he always this way when pursuing a woman? 'Ria, the day a woman can trap me into marriage is the day they bury me. How would you plan on doing it? Getting pregnant, perhaps ... our "friendship" would have to progress a little further before you could tie that lure, and all that would get you would be child support. Besides, I have no hang-ups about contraception. I'm quite willing to take care of it myself.'

Ria blushed at the mental images. She hadn't been on the pill, even when she was married. Her mother had died from coronary thrombosis and the doctor had told Ria she would be unwise even to take the slight risk oral contraception involved, with her family history. She blinked, re-focusing on the wilting asparagus at the end of the fork and blushed even harder.

The piercing blue eyes filled with laughter, had followed her capricious thought with ease.

'Perhaps I should have ordered oysters ... I think you'd better drink some cold wine, Ria, you're going to burst into flames any minute.'

'You really are awful,' she said, not knowing whether to laugh or cry at his teasing. She felt as she used to as a child when she had whirled around and around on the spot and then stopped, revelling in the sickening sensation of continued motion that made her feel giddy with delicious fright.

'You can trust me, you know, Ria,' he went on as her face cooled. 'I would never, never ask you to leave because of our personal relationship, whatever happened.'

'The question won't arise,' she replied with less confidence than she felt. 'But how can you possibly make such an unequivocal statement?'

'Because I know you're not the kind of woman who would make a nuisance of herself ... you have too much pride.'

'I would have said the same about you ... until now,' she said tartly, annoyed by the arrogance of his assumption. Did that mean that, once he had no more use for her in his bed, he would expect things to revert smoothly back to business-as-usual?

He smiled at that, quite unoffended. 'My God, you have a wicked tongue, Ria. Can't you see that all I'm doing is trying to be honest with you?'

'I see, and what about Marie Steele? Is she also expected not to make a nuisance of herself for the duration? Will you be just as honest with her?'

His eyes narrowed sharply. 'Marie is different.'

'Oh, really? And what does that mean, exactly?' she demanded sarcastically. He was using the same argument as Louis, except that the situations were reversed; this time it was Ria who was the 'other woman'. She was angry and at the same time bitterly amused at her anger. It wasn't wife *or* mistress that she wanted to be, it was both! She only hoped that there existed one man in the world who might want the same thing, or was she hopelessly out of date?

'It means that I don't want to go to bed with Marie,' he replied calmly.

Ria tensed her jaw to stop it dropping. 'But what happens when you get married?' she blurted out.

'I'm not going to marry her,' he said simply, and tilted his wine glass, regarding her flabbergasted face over the rim.

'But she's beautiful . . . and, and so *right*.'

'I meet a lot of beautiful women; I don't automatically want to marry them.' His voice was as dry as the wine. 'Was it you who started the marriage rumours?'

'Of course it wasn't,' she snapped, still not believing him. 'Everyone thinks you're going to marry her.'

'Why? Because she's so *right*?' He imitated the prissy word. 'And you, of all people, went along with it? God, Ria, do you really think that if I ever decided to get married it would be to a *child*?'

Put on the spot, Ria squirmed. She *had* thought that. It had put him at a safe distance to marry him off to someone so nice and eligible. It meant that whenever she had thought of him, it had been as someone else's, someone she liked. 'She's . . . she seems to be in love with you, and you—you haven't been seen around with anyone else for months.'

'Have you been keeping track?' He sounded annoyed. Ria didn't know whether it was the idea of her spying on him, or whether he was still irritated that she could think he wanted to marry Marie.

'No I haven't, but the rumour mill has.'

'Well, you can tell the mill that Marie is *not* in love with me—we're more like brother and sister, and I do a good job of fending off the fortune hunters. As far as her parents are concerned, I'm "safe".'

'Oh.' Ria eyed him dubiously, trying to imagine any parent thinking that a man like James Everett was safe. If she had daughters she would have been locking them up!

'Do I take it that now you know that I'm not under

contract you will allow yourself to look on me more . . . favourably?'

'No, you do not.' Ria reached for firmer footing. 'James, please, I *can't*; I mean I don't *want* to get involved with you.' She corrected herself hastily, aware that she wasn't projecting the image of cool unconcern that she had tried for. He was looking at her in a warm, intent way that made her feel flustered. Instead of acting like a woman entering her prime she was reduced to feeling like an awkward teenager. She had always sensed that he had the capacity to make her feel like this, that's why her disguise had been not only a means to an end, an end in itself.

'Ria——'

'Mr Everett, excuse me, but there's a telephone call for you at the desk.'

'For me?' James frowned at the waiter and then at Ria. 'Did you tell the switchboard where we would be?' Ria shook her head. 'It must be Gerry, then.'

Ria watched him stride away with immense relief. She should have known that open resistance was futile. She should have pretended to be desperately in love with someone else, or suffering from an embarrassing skin disease or something . . . He hated being chased but he liked *to* chase—he saw it as a kind of sport. Ria disliked the idea of being a quarry, she should never have broken cover, but oddly it wasn't as unpleasant as it had been with Louis. Louis had honour, but of a painful and oppressive kind. James was quite openly dishonourable and while he wound Ria into knots, at least he didn't make her feel staid or boring, however hard she tried.

'What is it?' James looked extremely grim when he came back to the table and picked up the jacket that he had left on the back of his chair.

'We'll have to go, I'm afraid.'

'Don't tell me we have someone else missing,' said Ria, forgetting her disturbing thoughts as James paid with his credit card and they stepped out into the sunlit street. It was hot and James merely swung his jacket over one broad shoulder. Ria, in a short-sleeved mint-and-white dress, had to almost trot to keep up with him.

'In a manner of speaking.' He suddenly scooped up Ria's hand in a hard grip and plunged across the street, dodging traffic. When they reached the other side he didn't let go of her hand and Ria couldn't pull it free. 'It's Tony.'

'Tony! You mean he's run away? From school?'

'He was actually suspended this morning.'

'Suspended! But why?' Ria was so shocked she stopped in her tracks and was almost jerked off her feet when James strode on one or two steps. He turned impatiently, tugging on her hand.

'A bunch of them were found with bags of glue in the playground. Stupid young idiots!'

'Are you sure Tony was actually involved?' Ria finally managed to pull her hand free. 'He might have been with them, but it doesn't mean he was *of* them.'

'Since he's disappeared we can't very well ask him, can we?' James snapped. 'Typical of Tony—he's a great one for avoiding responsibility.'

'That's not fair!' said Ria firmly. She stepped back against the solid marble pillar that marked the façade of a bank so that she wasn't impeding the flow of pedestrians. To her relief James moved, too, his face all scowling angles. She couldn't let him track Tony down in this mood, he would annihilate the boy. 'He's young and probably scared. Even if those boys were his friends I don't believe he would have joined in. He has too much character. The least you could do is calm down until you've heard his side of the story.'

'Calm down!' James glared at her. 'What the hell business is it of yours anyway? What makes you such a great judge of his character?'

Ria flared up at his sarcasm. 'I happen to know him quite well!'

The momentary silence between them was emphasised

by the noise of the traffic and the high-pitched buzz of a nearby pedestrian crossing signal. The summer sun struck the side of the bank and poured its heat down on to their bare heads—one dark, the other shot with flame.

'And just how well is well?' James said slowly, putting one hand on his hip, the other hitching his jacket more securely over his shoulder.

Ria braced herself against the pillar. His eyes were narrowing suspiciously as he absorbed the implications of her nervousness. Any moment he would reach the right conclusion himself. She felt it was better to confess it first. She lifted her chin.

'I haven't seduced him, if that's what you're implying,' she said with guilty defensiveness. 'We're friends, that's all. Just friends.'

CHAPTER SEVEN

AN instant before the explosion his eyes flashed an incredulous blue. Then came the slow, violent thunder. 'Oh—my—*God*!'

Heads turned. Footsteps slowed as people stared at the tall, furious-faced man scowling at the flushed red-head.

'You!' he hissed at her. 'Mya's been driving me up the wall for days about this bloody flame-haired temptress of Tony's, and all the time it was *you*!' Ria, who had only seen the iciness of his rage, was appalled and fascinated by the white-heat radiating from him now. He looked fit to murder. 'All this time you've been sitting there, butter wouldn't melt, while——' He bit off the snarl as he realised the attention they were getting. His hand snapped out to drag Ria around the other side of the pillar, into the shade. When a curious passer-by invaded their modicum of privacy, she was sent on her way with an imperious blue glare.

'James, let me go,' Ria whispered shakily. 'If you carry on like this someone's going to call the police.'

'Then you'd better talk, Ria, unless you want to be a chalkmark on the pavement.' The words were ground glass.

'Why don't we wait until——' She gave a tiny scream as he struck the side of the pillar with his fist and shoved his body threateningly close to hers. She hugged the pillar, feeling the fluted ridges of marble digging into her back.

'Quit stalling, Ria. Talk. *Now*. And make it good.' Each word blistered on her ears. 'How long has this been going on? Is that why Tony was so keen on my taking him to that restaurant on your birthday?'

'Of course not!' Ria hissed at him. 'We didn't even know each other then.'

113

'Don't lie to me, Ria, I've had it up to here with your lies,' he said savagely, the hand that held his jacket making a short, sharp cutting motion across his throat.

'I'm not lying,' Ria said, trying unsuccessfully to edge away from the taut, aggressive body threatening hers. 'It was the first time we ever met ... we exchanged Christian names and then, when you brought him into the office that time, he recognised me.'

'*I* didn't recognise you,' he accused grimly.

'You never really looked.'

'Well, I'm looking now!' And he was, up and down with a rigid fury. 'My *God*!' His fist slid down the pillar until it was level with her cheekbone, the hard tendons of his wrist just touching her skin. 'What is it about you, Ria, that sends men blundering about like blind idiots? If you've been confusing the boy with all those conflicting signals, no wonder he's in a mess!'

'I don't know what you're talking about,' Ria cried. 'All Tony wanted was company. He was lonely and a bit homesick. He just wanted someone to listen to him, to help him feel he was important, that's all.'

'Did you enjoy initiating him?' His voice flayed her like a whip. 'Did you enjoy sneaking around with him, encouraging him to defy his parents and forget his schoolwork?'

Ria bit the inside of her mouth to stop the angry words spilling out. Her was concerned about his nephew and, from his point of view, he had every right to be furious.

'There was nothing like that,' she said evenly. 'It was nothing to do with sex. Yes, he's been to my home a few times and lied about it, but I never encouraged him. You know what boys are—they exaggerate.'

'Nothing to do with sex?' His voice rose in disbelief. 'My God, you can't be *that* naïve! Everything involves sex when you're seventeen. The kid is a mass of adolescent urges and half-baked ideas about life. You kissed him the first time you ever saw him—that's encouragement enough as far as he's concerned.'

'I had no idea we'd ever meet again,' Ria protested weakly, knowing there was a grain of truth in what he said. 'I didn't even know he was your nephew until you appeared. It didn't mean anything.'

'It may not have meant anything to you, Angel Mouth,' he grated, 'but if the way you made me feel is anything to go by, the kid must have felt that the earth had just moved for him.'

Ria's jaw sank. The savagery in his voice was now intermingled with a more personal anger. His eyes dropped to her parted lips and she felt again the impact of his first kiss. She tensed against the pillar, pressing her open palms back against the cool marble. She felt like a witch, bound to the stake before her inquisitor, waiting for the first lick of flame, the searing heat that would consume her.

He drew a breath harsh and uneven. 'Witch,' he murmured, as if his thoughts had run along the same lines. His head shifted and for one shattering moment she thought he was going to kiss her right there in the street and she hungered for it. But the dark head jerked up at the last moment, though the smoky haze still lingered in his eyes, and in his voice.

'Is that the truth? No sex?'

'No s . . . sex,' she confirmed with a brilliant blush, the word sticking, all angles, in her constricted throat, aware that his anger had been altered, absorbed, by that moment of electric awareness. Her stumble drew his attention back to her mouth and she hurried on, huskily, to get it over with, 'I felt sorry for him. I . . . it really wasn't my idea. But he wanted to be friends; he found my address at your office and threatened that if I didn't see him——'

Fortunately he cut her off before she came to the awkward part. 'He'd tell me about your disguise. Yes, that would have appealed to this irritating propensity of his for harbouring secrets. I bet he enjoyed the thought of helping you put one over one me. I guess in his book that would come a near second to seduction.'

He seemed to relish the word and the way it brought a flicker of nervous awareness to her eyes. It mellowed him further, for experience, and a good deal of masculine confidence, told him that it wasn't the idea of sex with his nephew that disturbed her . . . and that left only one alternative.

'I did try to discourage him coming around,' she told him, her voice sounding surprisingly normal. 'But he was so persistent, and he had all these horror stories about what his friends were up to.'

'Not just stories as it turned out.' He studied her creamy upturned face. 'But you shouldn't have been surprised at his persistence. It runs in the family.' His fist came up, still closed but not clenched, to run down the side of her face, velvet on silk. It was the lightest touch, the faintest promise, but Ria went weak with the pleasure of it.

'James——'

'Ria——' He mocked her uncertain sigh. She was wearing her hair loose these days and he marvelled anew at how the sheer redness of it reacted so vibrantly with the passionate redness of her mouth, tempting him to lose himself in both. The freckles that were such intriguing indicators of her moods seemed to glow and he wondered with a sudden, pulsing curiosity whether they extended over the rest of her body, imagined kissing his way along the tiny, delicious, honeyed trails, wherever they might lead, imagined hearing her say 'James' in that husky voice, but as a plea not a protest.

Her eyes were wide as she stared at him, a deep, dark green like the sea under a shadowed sky . . . mysterious eyes. They made him want to force his way through the shadows, to plunder her every last secret. But the desire was tempered by cynicism. All too often a woman's mystery was of a man's own making, and the secrets not worth the effort of discovery. God, he was becoming as fanciful as his damned nephew . . .

'Come on.' He stepped back suddenly and began to

walk. 'We'd better go and see if we can find the Boy Wonder.'

Ria followed, dragging her feet, knowing that any moment his brain was going to start registering all the little inconsistencies, and throw out more curling qestions. Should she be defiant or defensive? Was this the moment for truth?

She thought of the way that he had looked at her, touched her, of how good it had felt. Did she want to put that in jeopardy, to put further suspicion and distrust between them? One part of her said she needed the defence. If he had kissed her there in the street she would have kissed him back, and kept on kissing him. His desire was as flattering as it was enticing and as dangerous as it was exciting. She could admit now that James Everett had always been an intensely attractive, sexy man but that up until now his attitude and her secret had combined to erect a mental defence against her acknowledging it. In her new state of vulnerability she knew that if she had been Ria Duncan instead of Ria Masson they would probably have already been lovers. But the old, carefree, Ria Duncan didn't exist. For her sons' sake she had had to be strong these last six years. When she was with James Everett she didn't want to be strong, she wanted to lean, to lose herself, to offer up responsibility to someone else for a change. She wanted to be free . . .

Ria came face to face with her guilt, the reason she struggled so determinedly against being attracted to James Everett. He made her resent her own children, her beloved boys. He made her wonder what it would be like to be unencumbered, a woman not a mother, to be free again to take pleasure where she chose and damn the consequences. Motherhood, for all its rewards, had its frustrations and sorrows too, and for the first time Ria longed to shed the entire suffocating skin.

'Incidentally, was Tony just trying to protect your identity when he spun that tale of a French widow, or was that some other infatuation entirely?' James asked casually as they entered the lift in the Plaza Building.

To Ria, in contemplation of deep, dark, unnatural thoughts, it was a vicious prod to her conscience. Her stomach lurched, not just with the motion of the lift and she paled visibly.

'Ria?' His eyes narrowed at her wordless panic, and Ria forced her mouth to open. The lift shuddered to a halt on one of the lower floors. The doors had opened when James slammed an open hand down over the *Door Close* button. A harassed-looking individual lept back just in time to save his foot from amputation.

'James, someone wants to get on.' Cowardly, Ria postponed the inevitable.

'Tough.' His mouth was grim as he contemplated her unease. '*Are* you French?' he rapped out. It was one of his techniques, to ask the easy questions first, to heighten the victim's tension about the ones to follow.

Ria braced herself. She might as well go down proudly. 'My husband was from New Caledonia.

A nerve flickered at the corner of his mouth. 'That's why you speak such fluent French?' he asked rigidly. Ria nodded, bewildered by his control. She had expected another explosion.

'Duncan isn't a very Gallic name,' he remarked, through teeth that were clearly clenched.

'It's my maiden name.' Ria watched the flickering nerve in awe, as if it were a sparking fuse. 'My married name is Masson.'

'Ria Masson.' He unclenched his teeth long enough to roll the vowels around his mouth. He still had his hand hard against the control panel and Ria noticed with a dry swallow that his knuckles were white with the pressure.

'My ... husband was killed in a car accident,' she said croakily, offering the gratuitous information as a kind of penance. The confined space of the lift was alive with crackling tension. Why didn't he get it over with, why didn't he snarl bitingly at her, fire her, *anything* but this terrible silence?

'When?' he asked with fearful control.

'S . . . six years ago.'

'Six years!' The tension snapped with his harsh exclamation. 'And you've never remarried? He must have been quite a man.'

He wasn't angry! Ria couldn't believe it. The fuse had stopped flickering and his mouth was curved in a faint smile even if his eyes remained curiously opaque.

'He was,' she said faintly, wondering if this was only the eye of the storm. 'But I haven't not remarried because of René, I mean, I mean . . .'

'I think I know what you mean. You rejected Louis because he was a pompous bore, not because he didn't enshrine the memory of your husband.'

Ria stiffened. 'I didn't exactly reject Louis, if you recall,' she pointed out.

This time his eyes did look amused. 'Come off it, Ria *Masson*, he was a wimp, and you knew exactly how he would react when you tossed down that mistress gauntlet.' His long dark lashes drooped as he added provocatively, 'If ever a woman offered herself to me in that tone of voice I'd put her across my knee before I put her on her back.'

'You wouldn't get the chance!' she flung at him, going hot and cold at the thought that he could have read her so easily. Was she that obvious to him? She was too appalled to blush at the other indecent thoughts his comment provoked.

'Of course not. When you offer yourself to me, I'm sure you'll be the soul of politeness.' He shook his head at her open-mouthed fury, and mused: 'What am I going to do with you, Ria? I cringe to think what else there is about you that I don't know.'

'Actually, James——' she began, finding a thin little voice hiding in her conscience.

'No!' She was taken aback by his violence. 'No. On second thoughts I don't really want to know, not right now. I have a feeling that I wouldn't like what you're going to say. Let's save the rest of the startling

revelations for another time.'

He took his hand off the control panel and they were both startled when the door opened to reveal the same irate individual waiting.

'Sorry. My secretary dropped her contact lens,' said James smoothly, moving Ria to make room for the mollified passenger. They rode up in silence, Ria's brain whirling. Was it a good or bad sign that he had stopped her telling him about the twins? He had seemed as genuinely reluctant to hear as she was to tell him!

Despite James' efforts to track him down Tony remained elusive. Ria half expected to find him on her doorstep when she got home, but Paul said there had been no sign of him. She made dinner for the twins, since it was Paul's night 'with the boys', and shuddered through a seemingly endless action adventure programme before shepherding them off to bed. Paul arrived home about ten and they had coffee together before Ria went upstairs to bed. She had just got out of the shower when Paul called up to her.

'Phone, *Chérie*.'

Ria streaked down the stairs in bare feet and a towel.

'Tony?'

'Who in the hell was that?' The growl made her toes curl into the hall rug.

'James!'

'I thought your husband was dead. Or was that Louis?'

'It was Paul.' Ria ignored his sarcasm. 'Have you found Tony?'

'And who, dare I ask, is Paul?'

'He lives with me. Tony hasn't shown up here. Have you tried his home again? What about the police?'

'He's here with me, Ria, he turned up an hour ago. He's just been walking around. We've had a talk, and I think we've managed to straighten a few things out. Other than being on the scene he had nothing to do with the glue incident.' He sounded brusque and uninterested.

'I knew it!' Ria exclaimed triumphantly.

'So tell me some more about this Paul. Does Tony know about him?'

'Of course he does.' Ria paused, suddenly realising the impression she had given. 'James, he's my father-in-law.'

'Is that legal?'

Ria mentally counted to ten. 'He lives with me, he doesn't sleep with me. It's not that kind of relationship,' she stated.

'I'm greatly relieved to hear it.' The warm masculine laughter didn't sweeten Ria's temper one bit. He was always accusing her of sleeping with someone!

'Well, bully for you!' She hung up on him violently and was halfway up the stairs before the telephone pealed again.

Paul appeared at the kitchen door, wiping his cup. 'I think you'd better answer it, *chèrie*, he didn't seem to appreciate speaking to me.'

'He thought——'

'I know; you were yelling.' He went back into the kitchen and closed the door as if he thought she needed the privacy. Ria thought she heard a chuckle through the panelled wood. She snatched up the phone.

'Ria? I'm sorry. I told you I can only absorb so many shocks in one day. Forgive me for teasing.'

'James——'

'Ah, I love it when you use that governessy tone of voice on me, it means I've got under your skin.' His teasing voice deepened as he went on, 'No, don't hang up. Tony would like to see you, and I thought it would be better if you came around here rather than vice versa.'

'Tonight?' Ria was startled.

'Tomorrow. For dinner. Did I get you out of bed?'

'No, I've just got out of the——' She stopped as a muffled groan vibrated in her ear.

'The bath? The shower? What are you wearing?'

She couldn't stop herself. 'A damp towel,' she murmured huskily.

'Oh, God. Perhaps you would like to come over

tonight. No need to change, just come as you are. I'll strip off too, so you don't feel uncomfortable.'

The drops of water trickling down between her breasts suddenly became cool, tracing fingers. She felt her nipples harden against the rough-soft towel.

'I feel uncomfortable just thinking about it,' she said involuntarily and he laughed softly in her ear.

'Uncomfortable doesn't begin to describe what I'm feeling. Tomorrow, at seven?'

'I don't think——' There was a vast difference between flirting with a disembodied voice and spending an evening with a man to whom she was already indecently attracted. She clutched the towel.

'Tony will be here to chaperon us. And he would like to tell you about his latest escapade . . . I think it would help cement the relationship between him and me if he knew that I wasn't going to make a fuss about him seeing you.'

'Oh, well, all right.' She bit her lip at the logic of it. Of course, verbal flirtation was quite natural to James Everett. It didn't mean anything momentous.

'I'll pick you up at seven then.'

'No, I'll get a taxi over, I'd prefer it,' she said hurriedly.

There was a moment's silence. 'Don't you want Paul to know that you're coming to dinner with me? Wouldn't he approve?'

'Of course he would. I mean, he's happy for me do to anything I want to,' said Ria thinking of the twins, who always insisted on making themselves known to her dates, few as they had been. She never knew whether they were exhibiting a childish protectiveness or making sure that this strange man knew who took first place in their mother's life.

'Good, then we'll see you tomorrow night. Look after yourself 'till then, Ria . . . and think of me when you unwrap that towel. If I were there with you you wouldn't need one, I'd dry you with my body and wrap you in my arms.

*   *   *

She thought of him all night and all Saturday morning whilst she and Paul got the boys ready for their first soccer game of the season. Her bed this morning had looked as though a herd of buffalo had stampeded through it. She had tossed and turned during the night unable to stop herself thinking of those evocative words. In the end she had given in and allowed herself to fantasise. She had done it before, but always before the man had been faceless—this time he had a very definite face, blue eyes that turned dark and sensuous in the pursuit of pleasure, hands that were skilled and gentle, a body that drove her to incredible heights of passion. The dreams were a blessed release from complex reality, though a modest corner of her mind was embarrassed by their intensity.

'I thought this was supposed to be a more gentle sport than rugby. Are they really supposed to be falling all over each other and the ball like that?' Ria winced as Michel took yet another tumble on the hardened pitch.

'You can't expect them to be World Cup standard in their first practice match,' replied Paul with a chuckle. 'They've barely worked out the rules of the game yet.'

Ria felt every bump as if she was out there playing herself, but she felt her throat tighten with pride at the determination on the twins' faces as they helped their team battle to a scrappy draw. They came streaking off the field when it was over, smelling of dirt and grass, bursting with the sheer delight of being alive and bombarding her with questions about their performance. Ria knew then, without a shadow of a doubt, that not even for a man who could make her feel the way James Everett made her feel would she be without her sons. Not for love nor money. They were as much a part of her as her red hair and freckles. She knew also that if she ever did have an affair, it would not be at the expense of her close relationship with her sons. She would not push them aside, or deny their existence. The man that she trusted enough to give her body to must accept her wholly, or not at all.

James Everett lived next to the rolling parkland of Auckland's Domain. As she paid off the taxi Ria could see the War Memorial Museum floodlit on its hill and, beyond the greenhouses and the trees of the park, the sprawling complex of Auckland Hospital. As Ria walked up the path she studied the house. It was of a similar vintage to her own, but several times the size, and generations of wealthy owners had preserved it in perfect condition.

She was shown in by a smiling middle-aged woman in an apron and led through a beautifully furnished hall and dining room to a spacious lounge.

'Ria!' Before she had time to greet either of the two men in dark suits and pastel shirts Tony had come forward to give her a warm kiss on the cheek, throwing a slightly challenging look at his uncle as he did so.

'Hello, Tony.' She smiled at him, trying not to look at the other man, feeling absurdly shy although she knew she looked her best in the smoky-grey chiffon dress with its drifting handkerchief panels.

'Ria.' Instead of kissing her on the cheek James opened his mouth over hers, drawing her body briefly against his, with his fingers almost completely encircling her waist. Over his head Ria's wide eyes saw Tony's surprise and chagrin and was furious with herself for blushing.

'And you've brought some wine, there was no need,' James continued smoothly as he released her and took the bottle from her numb fingers. His condescension melted when he saw the label and his eyebrows rose in self-mockery. 'Chateau Margaux? Extravagant, but perfect.'

'Actually it's from Paul, he has quite a collection.'

'And he sent you along with one of his best bottles, how kind of him,' James murmured softly as he took it away to open, but not before his smug blue eyes made her feel as if *she* had been the gift rather than the wine.

'Uncle James said I should apologise to you for being

a nuisance,' said Tony rapidly, in James' absence. 'Did *you* tell him I was one?'

'No, I didn't, but you did get us rather worried today. You're lucky J—your uncle held off calling your mother.'

'That was quite decent of him, wasn't it?' he said with studied indifference. 'He didn't yell at me or be sarcastic like he usually is. He spoke to the headmaster and they're not going to extend the suspension. Uncle James said——'

'I think you're old enough to drop the "uncle" these days, Tony.' James rejoined them, setting the open bottle of wine on the elegantly set dining table before moving back into the lounge. Ria could see from the glow on the young man's face that he was flattered by the suggestion of equality. James, it seemed, was rapidly reacquiring his status as a boyhood hero.

'James told the headmaster that he thought it would be a good idea if I stayed here next term, instead of boarding.'

Ria looked at James, surprised, and the corners of his mouth turned down fractionally.

'You put me to shame, Ria, with your caring. I wish there'd been someone like you in my life when I was seventeen. Sherry?'

'Dry, please. I can't imagine you at seventeen,' she murmured as she took her glass, noticing that he also gave Tony a small drink. So that was his magic formula—treat Tony like an adult and expect him to act like one. Adolescent pride would to the rest.

'I doubt you would have welcomed *me* into your life with open arms,' he said drily. 'I was the archetypal "wild one". Rude, aggressive, uncouth, no respect for authority and a burning ambition to get even with the world.'

'Were you in a gang?' asked Ria, trying hard to picture the sleek, sophisticated man lounging across from her as uncouth. Rude and aggressive she had no trouble in picturing!

'Baby, I *was* the gang,' he grinned. 'A single-handed crusade against the system.'

'So what happened to make you switch sides?'

'Oh, I didn't switch sides, Ria.' His eyes gleamed. 'It finally sunk through my thick skull that the only way to beat the system is from the inside. And along the way I discovered that the system could be used in ways I had never dreamed of. It amuses me to think that the men who rush *now* to invest their money in my companies would have set their dogs on me ten years ago. And the women who graciously smile at me would have crossed the street to avoid me.'

'James says that I can live here as long as I maintain my grades and don't cut school any more,' Tony broke in, tired of a discussion that didn't include him.

'It shouldn't be too difficult, providing you find out who your real friends are,' James said laconically, man-to-man. 'Guilt by association is damned unfair, but it's a fact of life. Shall we go through to dinner?'

The dining room, sectioned off the lounge by a chimney wall was small but dramatic. Red flocked wallpaper and silver grey carpet provided an exquisite background for the dark oval table set with silver and crystal. The meal was as fine as the sherry had been—cold soup, boeuf bourguignon—a perfect complement to the Margaux, and a rich chocolate mousse, all served by James.

'I have a cook-housekeeper, Mrs Parsons, who let you in, but she doesn't live in, so I often let her go before dinner. Thanks to the microwave revolution she never has to worry about the desecration of her beautiful meals.'

'Mmmm, much better than school food,' said Tony, packing away his second helping of mousse. He looked from his uncle to Ria and added, casually, 'Almost as good as Paul's.'

'Paul used to be a chef in the merchant marine,' explained Ria to a bland-faced James, wondering if it was her imagination that Tony was deliberately slipping in these comments to annoy his uncle. How much had he 'let slip' about Ria during that long talk yesterday?

'Don't worry, he didn't tell me any of your secrets, and I didn't ask,' said James, tiny blue devils dancing in his eyes as he traced the wrinkle in her brow.

'How very restrained of you,' she returned crisply.

'I prefer to discover them myself,' he said, with a softness that transfixed her spoon halfway to her mouth. 'The dance of the seven veils wouldn't be very erotic, would it, if all the veils fell at once?'

Ria's eyes were transfixed along with her spoon and she barely heard Tony's demanding, 'I love this wine, Ria. Can I have another glass?'

Without taking his eyes off Ria, James calmly removed the bottle from Tony's reach. 'I'm glad you like it, it shows you're developing *some* discrimination, but I think one glass is enough at this stage.' He released Ria from his spell as he returned his attention to his nephew. 'I don't mind you having the occasional glass at dinner, but there'll be hell to pay if your mother found out I was corrupting you with drink. She has no head for wine herself, and thinks no one else does either.'

The hint of male conspiracy softened the blow and Tony subsided. James was playing him like a master and as Ria adjourned with them to the lounge for coffee she had to admire his patience. From his point of view Tony had little to rebel against, compared to his own tumultuous boyhood. From several anecdotes Ria had discovered that James had never known his father, and that his mother had had a string of live-in lovers who had only barely tolerated her children. James' escape had been to take to the streets, to toughen his mind and body by creating his own challenges and beating them, his sister's had been to become a model daughter, never in trouble, anxious to be accepted by everyone. No wonder there was no real closeness now, except through Tony.

Encouraged by provocative comments, Ria found

herself drawn into an after-dinner argument on a wide range of topics. It was only when she noticed Tony's increasing silence that she realised what James was doing. By his very choice of subject—theatre, current affairs, politics—he was subtly emphasising the age and experience gap between Ria and Tony, simultaneously demonstrating the more equal relationship he was able to provide. Tony's occasional, rather sullen interjections, showed that the point was jabbing home with painful clarity.

Ria, sympathetic to James' motives, still felt a pang of disillusionment. But she had no right to feel annoyed, she hastily told herself, if Tony hadn't been here she wouldn't have come at all. It wasn't as if she *wanted* James to invite her to his home purely for the sake of her company. Well, she might want him to, but she wasn't as stupid as to expect it.

'It's late,' she said jerkily, putting her cup aside and realising with astonishment that it was, very late. 'I really must be going.'

'You had a wrap? I'll get it for you.' James departed with unflattering alacrity.

'You never told me that you and Unc—James were such friends,' Tony said accusingly, as soon as they were alone.

'There are a lot of things about me that you don't know, Tony,' Ria said firmly, knowing in all conscience that she couldn't sabotage James' careful efforts to encourage Tony to realise the limitations of their relationship. But neither would she deliberately hurt the boy. 'Friends aren't always obliged to tell each other everything.'

'But you and James, you're more than friends, aren't you?' he blurted, jumping to his feet. 'I'm not stupid. I've seen the way you look at each other.'

Ria rose jerkily, angry and embarrassed. My God, was she that transparent? She knew that James had sometimes looked at her across the table with a stomach-curling sexual hunger, but had she also let her deeper desires show? Had James seen it too?

'How dare you ask that?' she said quietly. 'I don't think that you deserve the dignity of an answer, friend or not.'

'What if I said I was in love with you?' he said, his skin tinging pink and a wounded-spaniel look entering his brown eyes.

'Even if that were true, Tony, and I hope it isn't because I value your friendship, even if that *were* true it wouldn't give you any rights over *my* feelings. Just because you love someone doesn't mean they owe you anything. Your feelings are your own responsibility, no one else's.'

He paled, but there was a sulky droop to his young mouth that told her that his talk of love had just been a way of punishing her for her apparent preference for his uncle. He muttered something stiffly and rushed rudely out of the room just as James returned.

'I hope you let him down lightly,' he murmured, dropping her fine lacy shawl around her shoulders.

Ria moved away glaring at him. 'You're as bad as he is—making all sorts of ridiculous assumptions——'

'Oh?' he grinned. 'Did he accuse you of being my mistress?'

'You know he did.' She marched stiffly out into the hall. 'That's what you intended him to think.'

'The thought had crossed my mind,' he admitted modestly. He caught hold of her elbow and halted her progress, saying gently, 'A little jealousy won't hurt him. If anything it'll do him good to realise that the world doesn't revolve around him.'

'He had no right to be jealous.' Ria glared at him in the soft hall lighting. 'Nor any reason.'

'I'm not speaking of sexual jealousy, though there are probably elements of that. I mean he's jealous of the attention that you're giving to me, and I'm giving to you.' There was a slight smile softening the firm mouth but his tone was serious. 'He's child enough to want to be the centre of our attention, and man enough to feel the challenge of another male. What he's feeling is quite natural, but also potentially dangerous. It wouldn't take much for him to think he was in love with you, and that would create a problem that I'm sure you don't want.'

'Is that why you invited me here tonight?' She turned her face away slightly, annoyed at herself for asking.

'Partly.' He stroked his hand up her arm to her jawline, grasping her chin and turning it back. 'But mostly because I wanted to do this . . .'

He kissed her mouth and her eyes and ears. His hands slid over her body, over the grey chiffon, shaping her, curving her boneless body against him. Ria felt an explosion of warmth inside her, a swelling ache that firmed her breasts in his hands and made her twist her hips towards him.

'God . . .' he bit her mouth lightly, 'I was thinking of this all through dinner.' He pushed her wrap off her shoulders and bent to kiss one rounded curve. 'Don't go. Stay with me.'

'No,' Ria moaned, pushing against his hard chest, trying to arch herself away from the knowledge of his eager arousal. The chiffon panels of her dress clung to his clothes, as her fevered senses clung. She felt an almost overwhelming urge to let herself sink into his embrace, to allow spontaneous desire to blossom unchecked, to retreat into the quiet, welcoming darkness of the house with him and lose herself in passionate urgency. But there was Tony upstairs, and the twins at home, and deep inside herself the slowly growing fear that she was emotionally as well as physically vulnerable to this man. It was better to have loved and lost than never loved—she believed that fervently—but *twice*? She couldn't bear to fall in love again and lose what she loved. And she didn't doubt that eventually, whether they were lovers or not, she would lose James Everett. He was too ambitious, too much a loner and, she feared, too much a man, for Ria.

'No, please——' She forced a desperate hand

between them, pushing against the mouth that roamed so deliciously along her demure neckline. James gave a muffled groan and for an instant Ria thought he was going to ignore her tortured plea, but then his head lifted and he read in her wide green eyes the unmistakable refusal. His body, rigid against hers, shook with a slight tremor as he slowly dropped his arms and stepped away from her. Ria shivered with the removal of his body heat, her mouth stinging as if he had whipped rather than kissed it.

'All right, Ria. This time.' His voice was thick and soft as he stood before her, all male, not trying to hide the physical effects of their shared passion. It took all his control to stand there and not snatch her back and force her to his will. He could do it; her mouth, her hands, her body had all admitted it, but her eyes showed a fear that could not be subdued by pleasure. It wasn't a fear of sex, of that much he was certain. It was something else, a mental resistance that he knew he had to conquer before she came willingly and eager to his bed. He wanted more than just her body, and until she was prepared to give him what he wanted, he must force himself to wait. But, God, it was agony!

CHAPTER EIGHT

A WEEK later Ria was beginning to wonder whether she had dreamt the brief, fiery display of passion. Since then James had been the epitome of politeness and made no attempts to see her out of strict office hours.

Ria caught herself watching him surreptitiously around the office, puzzled by his circumspect behaviour. She struggled to hide her pique, telling herself it was all to the good if he was regretting becoming any way involved with his secretary.

Still, his coolness infuriated her. What was he afraid of? Did he think that she might presume on their almost-relationship? Throw a tantrum like some of his past secretaries? Cry? Pester him with unwelcome attentions? He wasn't *that* irresistible. And he didn't even have the nerve to tell her to her face, to allow her to show him she didn't care!

'What kind of mood is he in, Ria?' She looked up from her brooding to see Gerry standing in front of her.

'Good . . . so far.' Viciously she slit open the next piece of morning mail. That was another thing. James had been so even-tempered this week that everyone was on edge, figuring he was building up to a big one.

Gerry held up his hands. 'Don't worry, I'm not going to change it. I just want an inconvenient day or two off.'

'Shooting on location, are we?' teased Ria. The actress had lasted longer than most.

'Fishing,' he grinned. 'Is he free?'

'As a bird.' Ria waved him in.

'Why, Ria,' he said slyly, 'I thought you'd have clipped his wings by now. You've certainly sweetened his disposition.'

132

The telephone rang as she frowned at his retreating back.

'Mummy?'

'Michel!'

'No, it's Jamie. I'm at school.'

'Are you sick?' Ria asked, with quick anxiety. Children were not usually permitted to use the telephone in the school office. 'Do you want to be picked up?' It was at times like these she felt most guilty about being a full-time working mother, in spite of Paul's competence.

'No, it's OK, the headmaster rang *Gran'père*.'

'The headmaster!' Ria groaned softly, it sounded like trouble.

'I just thought I'd ring you up while I waited.' The thin voice wobbled slightly.

'You mean you wanted to talk to me before Grandpa did,' said Ria drily.

'I hurt my hand,' Jamie protested, making her feel ashamed for her suspicions.

'Oh, darling, how? What happened?'

Having gained her sympathy Jamie couldn't help revealing his boyish triumph. 'I hurt it on Daniel's nose. We were playing karate. It bled *everywhere*.'

'Your hand?' Ria asked, horrified but thankful they had been playing and not fighting.

'No, Mummy,' came the impatient treble. 'Danny's nose. The blood spurted out real red, just like on TV.'

'Oh *Jamie*!' cried Ria, aghast, leaning her head into her hand, not noticing that the door to the inner office had opened and the two men were pausing, in conversation in the doorway. The conversation ceased at her exclamation.

'It's all right, really it is, but Mr Richardson said we'd had a fright and ought to go home. Caroline has to go home, too. Gosh, girls are dumb. She screamed and screamed and I didn't even hit her, just 'cos some blood went on her silly old shoes.'

'Oh, Jamie,' Ria groaned helplessly.

'I have to go now, Mummy,' said her son cheerfully. 'The sec'tary wants the phone. I love you, Mummy.'

'I love you, too, darling,' she responded with automatic warmth, deciding there and then that she was going to enrol the twins in a karate class. Let them learn that it was a sport of discipline and defence, not just a matter of flailing arms and legs, 'like on TV'.

She took the hand away from her face as she hung up, and found two pairs of eyes regarding her curiously across the room. One pair had a twinkle of amusement, the other was distinctly chilly. A blush swept over her face as she quickly picked up her pen and scribbled some gibberish on a piece of paper.

'As long as you make sure that Malleson is fully briefed before you go,' she heard James say curtly. 'I don't want Roberts getting the jump on us this close to the submission hearings.'

'Will do. And we've got ship-to-shore if anything urgent comes up.' Gerry left, whistling cheerfully, leaving a leaden atmosphere behind him. Ria bent her head closer to her papers, the nape of her neck prickling madly as she sensed James staring at her.

She risked a quick look. His hands were in the pockets of his navy trousers, a white shirt accentuating the breadth of his shoulders as he rocked slowly back and forth on his heels. Ria recognised the aggressive stance from long experience and stared desperately at the jumble of words on the page in front of her, feeling tension stiffen every sinew. Damn him, why should he look so accusingly at her after a week of practically ignoring her existence? It was none of his business if she chose to tell her son she loved him.

'Take a memo, *Mrs* Masson,' came the cold command. '"To all staff: The Management requests that personal telephone calls not be conducted during company time."'

Ria's head snapped up and she glared at him. His mouth moved briefly in satisfaction. 'And now, Ria, that I have your complete and undivided attention.

Who is he?' He walked slowly, purposefully over to stand in front of her desk, drawing his hands from his pocket to flex them on the outer ledge as he leaned towards her.

'Someone I love,' she threw at him defiantly.

'I gathered that. Every way I turn it seems that I fall over new men in your life. This is Jamie . . . he's your brother perhaps, or your father, or your second cousin once removed?'

His heavy sarcasm chipped away at a week of firmly cemented resentment. His eyes were ice-blue above the predatory nose, but the pupils were smouldering coals that ignited an answering flame in Ria. Gone was the businesslike employer. James was back with a vengeance.

'I don't have any relatives, except by marriage,' Ria snapped, trying to mask her stirring excitement. She had missed sparring with him, she hadn't realised how much.

'What, then? An old flame?'

'What's to stop him being a new one?' she said unwisely.

'Me.'

His smile was full of soft menace. He leaned further forward, so that his navy silk tie brushed her nervously clenched hands on the desk. She leaned back, her breathing accelerating, but his words pursued her.

'If he wants you, Ria, he'll have to go through me first.'

Ria's eyes sparked at his arrogance and she thrust out her chin, aiming with deadly accuracy. 'You may be able to organise my life within this office, Mr Everett, but out of it I do what I like, with whom I like.'

Instead of angering him, her blustering seemed to give him great satisfaction.

'Been getting to you, have I, Ria?' he insinuated softly. 'Been missing me, wanting me?'

Ria drew an angry breath. So it had all been a ploy, he had deliberately pretended not to be interested in order to soften her up. Well, she wasn't going to let him see how successful his underhandedness had been.

'Not at all. I've had Jamie to keep me company . . . not to mention Michel.'

His eyes narrowed fractionally at the new name but he continued silkily. 'They can't be very satisfactory, Ria, if it takes two of them to fill my shoes. Get rid of them, whoever they are.'

Ria stood up, flushed with anger. 'No!'

The gleam of amusement died out. 'I mean it, Ria, I'm not having anyone else between us.'

'Us! There is no *us*,' she cried, with a twinge of pain. Her sons would always be between her and any man. 'I thought you'd realised that this last week.' Her effort to turn the tables failed, for he caught the faint nuance that betrayed her chagrin.

'Liar. You seemed to want some breathing space, so I gave it to you. But I don't think you know *what* you really want.'

'Not you, that's for certain,' Ria lied furiously. 'I don't like to run with a crowd. You made the social columns this week . . . don't tell me you were minding *her* for a fond father!' It had hurt, the picture of a sleek, sophisticated beauty in his arms. It had reinforced her conclusion that he had transferred his attention to greener and more accessible fields.

'Jealous, Ria?' he taunted arrogantly. 'I had to fill the empty hours somehow. I'd much rather have taken you to bed than Roxy to a film première.' He injected an aggrieved note into his voice as he shifted lazily on his braced arms. 'I thought it was very unselfish of me to postpone our pleasure until you rid yourself of your doubts. I'm not generally such a patient man.'

'If you're talking about last Saturday night—' Ria rushed in frantically; at last the opportunity to make her little speech! '—that was a purely involuntary reaction——'

'A fluke?' He didn't let her finish, eyebrows rising as his mouth curved with delight at the weakness of her defence. 'Then I've fluked it three times already. I can't wait for the next!' His voice took on a husky quality that plucked at Ria's nerves. His lids drooped until his eyes were blue glimmers under dark lashes. 'You may be terrified of admitting that you're jealous, Ria, but I'm not. I'm a very jealous lover. What I have I hold. I don't want anyone else around . . . not even Tony, when he gets over his sulks. I don't like the way he keeps trying to touch you and I certainly don't like him kissing you.'

Ria shivered at the finely honed possessiveness, something in her responding even while she rejected it. 'And you talked about Tony being self-centred! What gives you the right——'

With stunning speed he moved and Ria found herself dragged by her shoulders until she fell across the desk.

'This . . . this gives me the right.' He kissed her, a bold, open-mouthed kiss of confirmation. Ria, her hips and thighs jammed against the computer keyboard on her desk clutched frantically at his chest, trying to regain her balance and twist her weight off three thousand dollars' worth of modern technology. He wouldn't let her, his mouth devouring her resistance, his heart thundering against the hot silk of his shirt.

Ria's fingers splayed across the powerfully seductive beat, her lips beginning to move under his in answering hunger. Her back arched painfully as he forced her head back further and Ria gasped against his mouth. With mind-blowing ease James moved his hands to her waist and the muscles of his chest and arms bunched and flexed as he swung her completely across the desk, sending papers flying, and set her down in front of him. Not breaking the fusion of their mouths he shifted back and kicked the outer door closed with casual disregard for the walnut finish.

'This gives me the right,' he muttered as he raised his head, pulling her submissive arms around his neck and wrapping one of his legs around her calves to draw her even closer. 'You see . . .' he nuzzled her bright hair,

'... you can insult me, tease me, ignore me, but you can't deny this feeling. You can lie about everything else but this. I realise now that I should never have let you go the other night; you're capable of convincing yourself that day is night. I should have staked my claim there and then and *proved* the rightness of it.'

'Not ... right ...' choked Ria, trying to fight the flooding warmth that threatened to overwhelm her senses. She had to think of her responsibilities, she couldn't let him just think he could take her whenever he wanted.

'Ah, Ria, how can you say that?' He bit her ear, his tongue teasing the lobe, questing for pleasure points. She gasped as he found one, heat streaking downwards as she sagged against him, her breasts vibrating deliciously to the quiet groan that rumbled in his chest. 'You like that, don't you?' he murmured, stringing kisses along her jawbone to her other ear which he nibbled contentedly. 'You like me to do this to your ears, it makes you soft and weak inside, it makes you want what I want.' He kissed her mouth, smothering her reply. 'Do you know what I'd like to do right now? I'd like to take you home with me and spend the rest of the day making love. I want to hold you in my arms and feel your skin on mine. I want the heavenly scent of you in my nose and in my mouth, I want to hear the sounds that you make as we make love. Do you scream, Ria? Do you cry out your joy or are you all quiet sighs?' His tongue slid along hers, hot and velvety, his hands stroking the taut arch of her back, his hips creating a gentle pressure between her thighs. 'I want to see you, Angel Mouth. I want to watch our bodies join and break apart, I want to feel the sharp sting of your mouth on me, the silky heat of your hands. I want to taste you, touch you, please you, rock you into sweet, sweet oblivion with me ...'

The throaty murmur sank into her sensitised ears, sank down, down, touching every part of her and exciting every part it touched. With his mouth and with his body he spoke a dazzlingly seductive language, inducing a lovely languorous feeling of weightlessness, as if her centre of gravity was James, and the universe revolved around them.

'James . . .' She sighed as he reluctantly and with effort slowed his sensual assault, finally resting a forehead damp with perspiration against hers.

'Ah, Ria, what you do to me . . .' He stared into the green glazed windows of her desire, finding there still a tissue-thin resistance that with all his expertise he couldn't quite penetrate. 'I'm not a boy, Ria, easily aroused or quickly satisfied. That's not my way. Granted I've escorted a great many women here and there, but lovers I can count on the fingers of one hand. When I was out there on the streets in my macho youth, sex was just another way to rebel. The girls I knew then weren't lovers they were symbols, they used me as I used them, to strike out at convention, to shore up the illusion that we were in control of our own lives and bodies. But I've long outgrown the need for those power plays. What I require now is an honest, adult relationship——'

'With no strings,' interrupted Ria her arousal fading slowly, painfully.

'Of course there are strings,' he chided quietly, 'inevitably there are those in any intimate human contact. I told you, I'm a jealous lover and you've shown an equal possessiveness. But legal strings, no. I'm not ready for marriage, I may never be. I'm not particularly interested in procreation for its own sake, and I'm too selfish to contemplate sharing my life that completely. But then, you've known that all along. I didn't think that was at issue here.'

'It's not,' said Ria, unable to lie in the face of his excruciating honesty. Slowly she extricated herself from his arms and smoothed her clothes with shaking hands.

'Then what is it that's holding you back?'

Ria shook her head helplessly. How could she explain her fears? He didn't want to share his life completely with her, but she was absolutely certain that he would expect complete loyalty and attention from her. It was unfair, but that's the kind of man he was. He would expect her to spend nights with him, to be free of commitments when he wanted her company. He wanted an affair and all the freedoms that it implied. He wanted her to 'get rid' of any other distractions in her life and concentrate on him.

James sensed her withdrawal and cursed inwardly. What had he said? For a moment he had felt on the verge of breaking through, but something had triggered her defences. She couldn't already be seriously involved with this Jamie, or Michel, whoever *he* was, not when she responded as passionately as she did to James. He tried to control his impatience. The waiting game had proved successful so far, he would continue it, rather than give in to the urge to beat her secret out of her!

With a sigh he let her go and walked over to open the office door.

'You'd better go and tidy up,' he said huskily, 'or the next person to walk in will think we've been having an orgy.'

Cooling her hot cheeks in front of the mirror in the rest room Ria saw what he meant. Her face was flushed and her lips looked swollen and tender. Her breasts seemed more prominent than usual beneath her chic lemon blouse, and when she put her hand protectively over them she was astonished at the wildly erratic beat of her heart. She felt a pain across her shoulders and chest and had difficulty catching her breath. All the symptoms of a heart attack, but not the fatal kind. Or perhaps it was, she thought wryly.

Then and there she knew she had to tell James about the twins, and soon. The longer she left it the more reluctant she felt, and the more reprehensible it was going to seem to James. She had been acting like a skittish virgin instead of a grown woman, making all sorts of excuses not to get involved with James when really there was only one. She was very close to falling in love with him. It would be disastrous, and she hoped that she never allowed herself to travel that final mile, but, equally, she wanted to explore the compelling attraction that she had discovered he had for her. She had been so busy telling herself what she *shouldn't* do that she had overlooked the things she *should* be doing: like enjoying life for its own sake instead of seeing it as an endless series of goals to be achieved. Security and stability were all very well, but in her determined pursuit of them Ria realised that she had sacrificed something along the way. She had let the weight of her responsibilities crush the adventurous spirit that René had so often teased her about. He had been the same; nothing ventured, nothing gained, might have been his motto and they had flung themselves wholeheartedly into living. Now, perhaps, she had a chance to recapture a little of that spirit, tempered by experience and a great deal more self-control, but still a part of her basic character.

Having at last resolved her vacillating doubts it was frustrating to be thwarted in her efforts to find a moment alone with James. There was a steady stream of visitors all day and, late in the afternoon, an urgent call from Wellington that had Ria scrambling to organise airline and hotel bookings.

'I'll be back tomorrow . . . I hope.' James farewelled Ria with a brief but thorough kiss in front of a grinning Gerry. 'We'll talk then,' he murmured into her pinkened face.

Ria watched him go with a flattening sense of anticlimax. She didn't need any more time to herself, she was anxious to get the awkward part of it over as soon as possible.

In the event it was three days before she saw James again. The tangle in Wellington took longer than he expected to sort out, and when he rang during office hours he sounded taut and under considerable pressure.

But in the evenings a different James called, her James. The first evening she was almost monosyllabic in surprise, but by the third she found herself opening up with warmth and teasing humour, freed as she was from the constricting penetration of his gaze.

Ria spoke with easy reminiscence about René, but carefully avoided any mention of the twins; she couldn't be such a coward as to break it to him over the telephone. James entertained her with stories of his misspent youth and flirted only lightly, as if he was afraid to frighten her off with any display of the possessiveness that had worried her before. The only time she felt a return of conflict was when they were discussing Tony, who had recovered sufficiently from his sullenness to 'phone Ria with the good news about his exam results. James had expressed his relief that his sister would have to restrain some of her complaints for another term.

'I have a feeling I might regret having let you shame me into taking pity on the boy. I fear I don't have the temperament to play father to other men's children.'

Ria told herself that it was just a casual comment about one particular situation. Besides, she wasn't going to ask him to play parent, only to see enough of the boys to reassure them that he wasn't going to steal their mummy away.

It was late on Thursday afternoon when he arrived back in the office, calling Gerry in for an immediate conference, throwing Ria a tired, half-apologetic smile that acknowledged the unspoken. Ria took copious notes of their conversation and answered any incoming calls on the phone on his desk. James chafed at the interruptions and when the telephone rang yet again he barked into it himself.

'Paul. For you.' He thrust the receiver impatiently at Ria, who rose uncertainly.

'Ria?' As soon as she heard his voice she knew. He used that tone so rarely, she *knew*.

'No.' She swayed on her feet, every nerve and muscle screaming a protest, a rejection of what he was going to say. Her face went pale with the effort of restraining the urge to babble wild questions as Paul sought for the words.

'I'm sorry, Ria . . .' he prepared her, 'Michel fell from the top of the slide, playing after school. He hit his head on the tarmac and knocked himself out. He's unconscious. We're at Auckland, the intensive care unit . . . Jamie's with me, I had to bring him, he was hysterical when I suggested he go with a friend's mother instead of in the ambulance.'

'Oh, God!' What little colour there was in her face completely drained away. Her heart felt as if it was pumping air. 'I'll be there as soon as I can,' she whispered, and dropped the receiver so that it hit the side of the desk and dangled limply to the floor. She felt herself begin to sink, her legs too weak to support her. It all came back to her . . . the smell of disinfectant, the muffled squeak of trolley wheels, the quiet, medical murmurs, the horrific sterility of the huge machines. The old nightmares rose up to mock her and her body was suddenly drenched with icy sweat.

'Ria?' Gerry was there, putting his arm around her, only to be violently thrust aside.

'Ria?' James lifted her shaking body, gripping her tightly. 'What's happened, Ria? Is Paul hurt?'

'No!' She shook her head violently, finding her strength. Her son . . . her son was dying. She wrenched herself free of James. 'I have to go, I have to go!' She ran, stumbling, to the outer door, not even stopping for her bag. All she knew was that she had to get to Michel, she had to see him.

'You're in no state to go anywhere.' James caught up with her, his voice coming from far away. 'I'll take you . . . where to?'

'The hospital, the hospital!' She screamed at him for being so stupid, tears beginning to pour down her face. 'Michel's hurt, he might be dying! Let me go!'

She lashed out at him, and James, almost as pale as she, took the blow without flinching. He spoke over his shoulder, not taking his eyes off Ria's anguished face.

'Hold the fort, Gerry. I'll call. Come on, Ria.' He took her by the elbow and steered her out to the lift, shielding her distress from passing workers and ruthlessly commandeering the lift for themselves.

Ria was scarcely aware of the ride to the hospital. She sat stiff and white, shedding silent, rigid tears feeling sick with fear, and angry at the unfairness of it. She couldn't lose Michel, she *couldn't*. She moaned, like an animal in pain, and James' knuckles clenched white on the wheel as he ran a couple of red lights. Ria hardly knew he was there. At the hospital she ignored him, running from the car before he had switched off the engine, asking at the information desk in a shaking voice and taking the stairs instead of waiting agonising minutes for the lift. James followed her frantic footsteps with grim-faced purpose and reached out to catch her when twice she stumbled in her haste. She pushed his hands away angrily, as if he was trying to stop her reaching her son, telling him to leave her alone. But still he followed.

At last she saw Paul, at the end of a long, pale green corridor. He was alone, his shoulders slumped, looking small and old. Ria's fast walk broke into a run.

'Paul!'

He gave her a haggard smile. 'He's still unconscious, *chérie*. They're waiting for the X-rays now. The doctor thinks there might be some pressure building up.'

'Oh, God!' Ria swayed, felt a solid warmth support her from behind, a steadying hand on her waist that this time she didn't reject. 'Oh, Michel! why did it have to be Michel? Can I see him?' She looked around. 'Jamie! Where's Jamie? *Where's Jamie?*' She had to reassure herself, to see Michel's mirror-image, to hold him.

Behind her, James felt the words like the thrust of a white-hot poker.

'He's with one of the nurses, he was still very upset.' Paul hesitated, his dark eyes flickering past her and up. 'I'll go and get him. And I'll ask if you can see Michel.'

'I'll stay with her,' James assured the older man with

a quiet authority that helped ease a fraction of the tension in Paul's grey face. 'I'm James Everett.'

'She hates hospitals, since René . . .' Paul murmured and blue eyes met brown in perfect understanding.

'I'll take care of her.' The slight hoarseness in James' voice gave the words the intensity of a vow, and Paul nodded gratefully as he moved away.

'He's going to die, isn't he? He's going to die!' Ria whispered frozenly, unable to hold it any longer.

Without letting go of her James moved around to the front of Ria and took her icy hands in his, chafing them gently. She looked at him dazedly, a source of warmth and badly needed strength. He looked so calm, so confident, holding her stricken gaze with unwavering blue eyes.

'All we can do is wait, Ria. Wait and hope.'

'But I don't want to wait,' she cried frantically. 'He'll die while we wait. Like René. We waited weeks, but René still died. Michel's going to die, too!'

'Don't, darling, don't make it worse.' He drew her cold hands further into the warmth of his chest. 'The doctor is doing everything he can, Ria, you must believe that.'

'I don't know if I can.' Her voice was full of tears, of hopeless tears, but her eyes were frozen.

'Then I'll believe it for you.' He held her gently, willing her to accept the little comfort that he could give. Fiercely he wanted to take on the pain on her behalf, to keep her safe from harm. She looked so utterly helpless, so scared, so vulnerable. His arms tightened involuntarily as she buried her face in his shirt-front. He could hold her for ever, fend off the world and all its ugliness if she would only let him. James, who had never had anyone anguished, or even particularly worried on his behalf, felt awed by the shattered woman in his arms. What love she must feel, to feel such grief. How could he possibly compete with it?

A bleak emptiness entered his eyes. Even now, it

wasn't him she wanted to turn to in her blind need, it was his namesake ... the unknown Jamie. For all the solace James could offer her he might as well not be here. But, God damn it, he would offer it regardless!

Over Ria's head he saw a small boy come out of a door, followed by Paul and a uniformed nurse. The boy had great dark eyes that fixed on James accusingly and shimmered with tears. Realisation hit him the instant the boy began to run.

'Mummy!'

'Jamie!' Ria fell into a crouch, hugging the small figure impossibly close, hungrily taking in the sight and sound of her son. She touched his face and his hair, and held his thin, shaking shoulders.

'I tried to catch him, really I did. I should have tried to stop him climbing—*j'aurais dû l'arrêter. J'ai couri vers lui mais il est tombé tout d'un coup! Je n'ai su que faire!*'

'Hush, darling, *doucement, mon fils.*' Ria rocked him, consoling him with soothing phrases of love in both languages, finding the strength she had lacked in the comfort of another. 'It wasn't your fault, *mon petit*, it was an accident. You did fine, just fine and now we must be brave for him.'

'His eyes were all funny,' he sobbed. 'Is he dying, *Maman*? Are we dying?'

Ria closed her eyes on the pain. Whatever she was feeling, little Jamie was feeling tenfold. The twins were like two halves of a whole, born of the same cell; sometimes he and Michel even shared the same thoughts.

'We won't let him die.' She kissed his silky head. 'We won't let him die. But we must be very, very brave. We must be ready when he needs us.'

The idea that he could somehow help seemed to calm Jamie, though his small face was still hurt and bewildered with its streaking of tears. Holding his hand tightly Ria rose slowly to her feet, looking past James' blank, shocked expression to where a doctor had come quietly out from one of the rooms. All Ria's being was concentrated on her grave approach and she prayed as she had not done so in six years.

CHAPTER NINE

RIA sat motionless, gripping her son's small, limp hand. Night had merged with day in the small, windowless room. She had little idea of how long she had maintained her vigil. Doctors and nurses made their endless rounds, coffee and food trays were brought in and taken away again almost untouched. Sometimes Jamie and Paul were there; she was even vaguely aware of James Everett. But even his commanding, demanding presence didn't succeed in penetrating her numb daze. All her energy, every particle of will, was directed towards her unconscious son. *She* was his link to the world, she would make him come back to it through sheer willpower. So she sat, unmindful of the concern being expressed about her. Sat and waited.

Dr Bradley had been explicit, yet vague in the way of doctors. 'There's a hairline fracture, but no apparent pressure build-up inside the skull. Naturally it's a matter of concern that Michel hasn't regained consciousness, but on the positive side he's breathing without a respirator and his vital signs are good.'

'Then why is he still unconscious?' Ria had whispered as she first gazed upon her son, pale and fragile in the large bed.

'We know a lot about the brain and its workings,' Dr Bradley had said, her pleasant face showing the effects of a long tour of duty, 'but there's also a lot that is still a mystery. We've done all we can, now it's just a matter of watching and waiting.'

The mother in Ria bitterly resented the doctor's cautiousness. The echoes of the past became louder. Why did doctors always assume that relatives were incapable of coping with medical speculation? She wanted to *know*. What were Michel's chances—eighty per cent? Forty? Might he never wake up? Might he spend the rest of his life in limbo? Ria needed to know the worst. It couldn't hurt her, not when her emotions were frozen into this blessed numbness. Anything was better than not knowing.

She was proud of her self-control, not seeing it, as others did, as dangerous bottling-up of her grief. When René had lain in a coma Ria had grieved openly and been comforted, but this time she was afraid of letting go. She *had* to be strong, for Jamie's sake. She mustn't frighten him with the savage anger and fear that seethed inside her.

Fiercely Ria rejected all attempts to pry her away from Michel's bedside. Paul brought in a case and Ria lived, ate, slept within the confines of her sterile prison, though actually she did little of any of them. The narrow bed against the other wall remained unused. She was afraid that if she relaxed her vigilance Michel might slip away from her.

'Ria?' She recognised the voice and didn't turn.

'He's still the same,' she said flatly, too weary even for a conventional greeting.

James Everett came across the room to stand beside her. After looking briefly at the motionless figure on the bed he turned his gaze on Ria, noting the stiffness with which she held herself, the burning intensity in her eyes, the locked fingers that linked her to her son.

'I know, Dr Bradley told me. You've been here for three days now.'

'It's good of you to visit.' Ria pushed away the thought that the longer Michel remained unconscious the more chance there might be of permanent brain damage. She wanted to know the worst, but she was deathly afraid of the knowledge.

'I'm not just visiting. I picked up Jamie from school and brought him and Paul over.'

'Oh.' She looked up, then wished she hadn't. James' face had a hard, cold cast. Panic fluttered briefly ... that expression usually meant that he was going to be brutally unpleasant. 'You didn't have to do that.'

A muscle twitched in his cheeks. 'Yes, I did.' His voice was tight with self-restraint. 'Do you know how difficult it's been for Paul, rushing back and forth, worrying about Jamie and you as well as about Michel?'

'Of course I know,' she said defensively. Was he suggesting it wasn't difficult for her? She stared, dry-eyed at her son. She was the one who sat here, night and day, taking on the full burden of worry. Paul and Jamie understood, they knew that for the moment, Michel must come first.

'In fact I've been bringing them down every day. They've been staying with me, since it's closer to the hospital. I drop Jamie off at school every morning on the way to work. His teacher says he's a little unsettled, but that he seems to be coping very well, in the circumstances.'

Ria looked at him blankly. What did he want? Gratitude for his good deeds? No one had asked him to get involved. Why did he bother, since it obviously made him so angry? He was staring grimly at her, as if he wanted to hit her. How could he expect her to think about mundane, day-to-day things when Michel could be dying?

'Well, thank you for——' she began resentfully, her head beginning to ache with the effort of concentration.

'I don't want your thanks,' he snapped tautly. 'Don't you think it's about time you stopped pushing everyone away? Other people love Michel, too, you know, don't you think it's about time that they were allowed to show it?'

'I don't know what you mean,' Ria croaked, stunned by the attack.

'I mean that Jamie and Paul are feeling shut out. They need to spend time with Michel, too. But you won't let them near him, you sit there wallowing in your own anguish and forgetting theirs.'

Ria felt the wall of numbness that surrounded her tremble from the blow. She let go of Michel's hand

and rose, swaying, to her feet, white with pain and anger.

'Mr Everett——' She hadn't even noticed that Dr Bradley had come at the same time as James and was now laying a restraining hand on his sleeve.

'No, doctor, she needs to hear this. Paul and Jamie need to feel they're helping just as much as you do. Let them spend a few nights with Michel, let them share the comfort of *doing* something instead of being relegated to the sidelines.'

'No!' Ria recoiled from the suggestion. 'I've got to stay, I've *got* to!' She shook with the effort of making him understand. 'He's my son, I can't leave him, he's my son——'

'He's Jamie's brother, his twin, and Paul's grandson. He doesn't belong exclusively to you, Ria.' James' voice was hoarse with the pain of hurting her, but Ria heard only his implacability.

'You don't understand,' she choked, rage releasing some of her trapped emotion. She felt as if she was exploding, floating above the floor. She struggled against the tiredness that suddenly hit her like a stone wall, smashing into her precious barriers of self-control. She hit out, desperately, 'Go away! I didn't ask you to interfere, I didn't ask you to come here, go away!'

'I can't do that, Ria, I can't let you carry this by yourself,' he said, quiet now that she was shaken by storm.

His gentleness was like the slash of a knife. 'You don't know what it's like,' she cried, 'how can you? You haven't got any children. How can you understand? You don't know ... you don't know ...' Her voice sank to a whisper and the doctor exclaimed quietly in the background but James Everett merely stepped forward and wrapped Ria in his arms.

'I know that you're hurting, Ria, and I know that you can't go on like this. You hardly know what you're saying or doing. You need food and rest.'

'I can't leave,' she whispered against the soft grey

linen of his suit, fighting against the desire to sink into his arms and never leave. For days she had been cold, oh, so cold, and suddenly she felt a warmth creeping up over her. The hard, enveloping body was secure and strong, it pulsed with life, with hope.

'Come on, honey.' The words stirred the damp hair at her forehead. 'Don't fight me. What use are you going to be to Michel like this? You need to recoup your strength. You'll only be five minutes away from the hospital, if there's any change; let someone else take charge for a little while.'

To his logic and persuasive softness the doctor added her assessment. 'And it might be valuable to Michel, too. You've been reading aloud and talking to him for days, perhaps a change of voice might help trigger something. You said that he and Jamie have a very strong bond; perhaps the special awareness that twins share might be able to penetrate his subconscious.'

Enfolded in James' arms, Ria felt her resistance draining away. Everything was a confusing jumble with only the hard core of pain discernible. Suddenly every limb was weighted, except her head. That felt light, dizzy, separate from the rest of her body. Stumblingly she allowed James to lead her out into the corridor and summoned the strength to give the waiting Jamie a hug and kiss.

'I've brought my suitcase with my 'jamas in,' he said, showing her proudly, 'and some books to read to Michel, and a Space Wars tape to play for him ... it's his fav'rite.'

'I'm lucky to have you to take over, aren't I?' Ria blinked hazily at him, ruffling his dark hair, feeling a welling guilt that she had let him down when he most needed a mother's closeness and reassurance. She had two sons, and she loved them equally.

'Come on, Ria, you're out on your feet.' James drew her away firmly, but with infinite gentleness.

'You will call if anything happens?' she asked anxiously of a drawn, but relieved, Paul.

'I promise. Don't worry about anything, Ria, James will look after you.'

James did, but Ria didn't recall a minute of it. Her body defeated her, and she fell asleep almost as soon as James tucked her into his luxurious car. When she awoke, it was broad daylight.

Ria blinked at the strange light-patterns on the ceiling. Her bedroom never got morning sunlight. Then she registered that it wasn't morning, the sun was high in the sky, and this wasn't her room. James. She was in James Everett's house. She pushed herself up, grimacing at the sour taste in her mouth and the muffled thumping in her head. She frowned down at her peach-coloured slip. She didn't remember getting undressed. She didn't remember anything after leaving the hospital.

'Ah, you're awake at last.' Ria looked blearily at the friendly face that bustled into the room, recognising its owner as the woman who had let her in the night she came for dinner. 'I'm Mrs Parsons,' she confirmed. 'Mr Everett told me to look in on you every now and then. There's been no change in your little boy's condition ... I'm sorry about your trouble, it must be terrible for you. Now, Mr Everett said you'd probably want to hurry on over to the hospital ... he's arranged for a taxi for you, but he said that first you had to eat. So when you're ready, just come on down to the kitchen.'

It was a long time since Ria had felt so mothered. Mrs Parsons showed her the wardrobe and the drawers, filled with clothes that Paul had brought over for her, and insisted on running a bath, chattering all the while, blessedly not expecting any reply. Ria let the words flow over her and, after the other woman had withdrew, slid into the bath with a long sigh of weariness. She had slept for nearly twenty-four hours yet she still felt sluggish. She lathered her hair and soaped her body slowly, enjoying feeling clean for the first time in days, but the hot water seemed to drain what little strength she had. She dressed slowly, trying to shake off the dizziness, and then found her way downstairs to the kitchen, where Mrs Parsons fussed over her while she ate a light lunch of soup and scrambled eggs.

'Mr Everett said something light,' Mrs Parsons chattered. 'He was worried that you hadn't eaten for days. That boy of yours is a good eater. I must say, it is nice to have a child around the place ... this house needs filling. He should get married and have some of his own—he'd make a splendid father. He and your Jamie got on like a house on fire.'

Ria frowned over her eggs as Mrs Parsons' conversation skipped back and forth over a variety of subjects in a short space of time. She hardly thought a few days' practice would qualify James Everett as good father material. Jamie had been subdued by his brother's accident, and was no doubt on his best behaviour. And James ... well ... she shied away from thinking too much about his behaviour. The time must surely come when he would tax her about her deception and at the moment she felt too weak to marshal her feelings about him into order. She was at once resentful and grateful for the way he had taken charge, but what did it mean to him? Was he just fulfilling a moral obligation to a valued employee? Or was it more than that? Did he still want her, or had the discovery of the twins' existence changed his attitude entirely? Now that he had seen her as a worried parent, irrevocably tied down to her responsibilities, would he still see her as a desirable woman? Perhaps now he just felt sorry for her, and this apparent caring was just a way of assuaging his guilt.

At the hospital apprehension tightened her stomach as she approached Michel's room. But Mrs Parsons' report had been depressingly right. Michel lay just as she had left him and Paul sat reading at the bedside, the radio on the locker playing quietly.

'I'm sorry, Paul,' she apologised, slightly shamefaced, after they had exchanged greetings. 'Why didn't you say something to me ...?'

'You were being a mother, *chérie*, I couldn't chastise you for that,' he replied with a loving shrug. 'I think perhaps James was the only one who saw clearly what you were doing to yourself. I said I wouldn't force you to leave against your will ... he said he'd take the responsibility.'

Ria stiffened. She didn't want to be a responsibility. 'It wasn't his place——'

'He earned his place, Ria,' Paul told her quietly. 'He could have turned around and walked away after he brought you here, but he didn't. He's a generous man, *chérie*, and I'm not just talking about the material help he's provided. He's spent a lot of time with Jamie over the past few days. You've always said how hard he works, but he has put business second for the sake of one uncertain little boy. He has made us feel welcome in his home, and even enjoyed the company, I think.'

'But why? Why is he doing all this?' Ria asked, more to herself than to Paul.

He looked thoughtful. 'That's something you'll have to ask him, *petite*,' he murmured.

'I will ... later, when Michel ...' Ria trailed off, and was utterly astounded by Paul's added:

'Don't hurt him, *chérie*. He's a good man.'

Ria pondered that in confusion as she sat for a while beside Michel. How could she possibly hurt James Everett? What had he said to Paul to make him think such a thing? Did Paul mean his ego? His pride?

The thoughts scurried around and around inside her head, bringing back the ache. Just when she needed most to concentrate on her family there was James, distracting her, churning up new and strange worries, making her feel desperately vulnerable.

She felt awkward, self-conscious, when James came in later, hand-in-hand with Jamie. She felt a disturbing pang of jealousy when she saw them together and wasn't sure which one she was jealous of ... James for having so obviously gained some of her son's precious affection, or Jamie for having the childish freedom to cling to James' strong hand and demand, and receive, his gentle attention. As a result she was lavish with her maternal love and short and sharp with her employer. Tolerantly he allowed her her moment of revenge, recognising her need for assurance.

'Uncle James and I went to MacDonalds' last night,' Jamie informed her, happily unaware of the tension stretching above his head. 'I told Michel all about it when we came back. Uncle James said that when Michel's better we can all go together.'

Ria's eyes fluttered to the watchful blue ones, unaware of the silent plea.

'That's if you'll let me take you,' he murmured softly, as if he had no doubts at all that Michel would soon be munching a Big Mac with the rest of his family.

'Of course, we'd love to come,' Ria replied, with a faltering smile, her resentment draining away. James seemed to know exactly the right words to undermine her resistance.

'After we had our hamburgers we went to a video parlour and Uncle James scored nineteen thousand points on Astropilot. He'd never even played it before but he got the top score,' her son offered in awe.

'Really?' Ria asked faintly, trying to adjust to this new aspect of James Everett.

'He even beat me. I don't think he's a beast at all!'

'Jamie!' Ria blushed to her ears, as it suddenly occurred to her that Jamie could have revealed all sorts of embarrassing facts about his mother. 'I hope he hasn't been a nuisance,' she said hurriedly, avoiding the amused blue gaze.

'On the contrary,' James murmured, enjoying the look of confusion on her face. It was the first time in days he had seen her without the lines of tension tautening her face ... except this morning, in sleep, when she had looked soft and untroubled, as if she belonged there in his house, under his protection. 'Your son has been a delight. You must be very proud of him.'

'I am.' A lump rose in her throat. It shook her how much James' sincerity meant to her, how much she cared what he thought about those she loved.

'Then you won't object to his spending another night here? Please, Ria, you need at least one more night's sleep.'

Ria found herself giving in to his request, where an order would have had her rebelling. James disappeared for a few hours and came back, just before dinner, to collect her. Meekly getting into the car Ria found herself wondering, for the first time, what was happening outside, in the real world.

'How are you managing at the office?' she asked tentatively of the absorbed profile.

'Freeman is standing in for you.' He threw Ria a slight smile. 'She squawked a bit about the change in routine but after she met Jamie she went like a lamb. That boy has a way with women . . . you should see him charm the nurses.'

'Like his namesake,' Ria muttered under her breath, but he heard.

'He was quite fascinated that our names are so similar. No more fascinated than I, of course, when I found out that your lovers were really your sons,' he added silkily.

There was a short silence. Ria wondered at the lack of emotion in his voice, 'I *was* going to tell you, but, well . . .'

'Am I really the beast you told the twins I was? Did you really think I would fire you?' Was that reproach she detected?

'I don't know,' Ria said huskily, staring out of the window as they wound through the tree lined Domain road. 'You do tend to be a bit unpredictable temper-wise.'

'But not inhuman, you should know that by now.' He drew up in the driveway of the house and swivelled to look at her. 'Or perhaps you were more frightened of my reaction as a man, rather than as an employer.

Don't you realise, Ria that it only makes you more desirable? To know that you have carried children under your heart, loved them, nurtured them. God knows, you must have struggled to support them at times . . . and I have nothing but respect for the fine job you've obviously done. It makes me feel . . . inadequate . . . I who have loved no one, who never knew what it was to bleed for someone else. Ria, you make me realise how little, for all my riches, I possess.'

The words made her tremble, the envy in them was so genuine, the sense of emptiness so real. They played on her tender sensitivities, the rawness of her emotions. She wanted to open her arms and draw him to her breast, to her heart. Could he be as vulnerable, in his own way, as she was? Did she really have the power to hurt him?

It was a strange evening. As if he sensed the agitation that his soft confession had aroused, James concentrated on making his company as relaxed and undemanding as possible. He even managed to make her laugh a few times, teasing her into appetite for the delicious meal, and dealing gently with a telephone call from Tony, enquiring about the patient.

'Time you were in bed, Ria,' he said firmly, catching her in mid-yawn over her coffee. He must be tired, too, she thought, working as well as doing all that he was for her and Paul.

'I'd offer to come up and undress you, but I don't think you'd be as compliant about it as you were last night,' he added wickedly, chasing her out of the room on a blush as she realised what he meant. It didn't help to tell herself that he must have seen plenty of half-dressed female bodies. This was *hers*.

After her previous night's sleep the dreams came as a shock. They plunged her into a world of dark despair and hopelessness. She struggled to reach out to Michel, to help him, but something was holding her back. She screamed and fought, but she couldn't escape, couldn't move, tentacles of fear wrapped suffocatingly tight around her.

Then suddenly they weren't tentacles any more, but arms, warm and strong and familiar, pressing her against a hard, naked chest, where soft curls absorbed her racking sobs.

'Ssshhh, Ria, it's me. It's James. It's all right, darling, I'm here, I won't let you go. Ria . . .'

'You went away,' she sobbed brokenly, not sure whether she was talking to René or Michel; not knowing what she meant, only needing to be held, to be loved.

'I'm here now. I won't leave you,' came the husky promise as she was rocked in the warm haven. But she couldn't stop the tears. The dam had finally broken and the sobs came wrenching from her chest, along with all her disjointed fears about death, about losing someone else that she loved.

For an age she cried, until the warm chest was damp with her tears, until the sharp, jagged pain become a dull ache, until the stormy torrent of emotion was spent.

'It hurts, James, it hurts,' she moaned, burrowing her face into the satiny softness of his upper arm as it held her close.

'I know, darling, I know.' James held her trembling body, his hands stroking her back through the thin white lawn gown. He felt her pain acutely, and he felt a fierce pleasure that she knew, even in the nightmare confusion of tears, who it was she had turned to. She had been asleep when he came in, fighting the horrors alone, but when he had taken her in his arms she had cried his name.

'Make it go away, please, make it go away,' Ria begged desperately, clutching him tighter, feeling his life beating into her through the muscled wall of his chest. He could make her forget. James could blot out the pain, James could help her escape from reality for a little while longer.

'Ria . . .' He responded with comforting male assurance. His mouth moved over her damp face, pressing against her eyes, her nose, her mouth, in soft, comforting caresses. They were soothing, asexual kisses, and they made Ria obscurely angry.

Her hands moved at his waist, just above the silk pyjama trousers, and her mouth opened as she sought his wandering lips. She didn't want to be petted like a child, she wanted his strength, his virility ... she wanted him to blank out the ache inside by making her ache in other ways.

She pushed her tongue against his teeth, raking her nails over the taut skin of his stomach. He sucked in a harsh, rattling breath.

'Ria——' His hands pushed at her upper arms as she wound them around his neck. Arching against him she felt her breasts swell against the lace edging of her nightdress.

'Heal me, James, help me ...' she pleaded huskily, pulling him down towards her so that his feet left the floor and one hand braced against the bed to stop himself falling on top of her.

'Ria, don't,' he groaned as he looked down at her in the pale moonlight. Her hair streamed over her naked shoulders, the thin straps of her nightdress drooping invitingly down her arms, the lace barely clinging to the fully rounded curves. In the shaft of light that fell across their bodies he could see the rosy half-circle of a nipple peeking at him, begging for his touch. 'Oh, God, Ria, you don't know what you're doing,' he breathed, as the ache in his loins intensified. He couldn't take advantage of her weakness. He would despise himself in the morning ... and Ria would hate him.

'I know ... *this* is what I'm doing ...' Ria muttered, placing nibbling kisses against the defensive arch of his throat. 'And this ...' She kicked away the sheets and twisted against his braced arm so that James sagged against her. Feverishly she wrapped herself around him, trapping him in an erotic confusion of silk and lace and velvety skin, feeling the involuntary response of his body and the quick movement he made to hide it.

'You want me . . . you said you did . . . you want me,' she said exultantly, brushing the back of her hand against his arousal so that he made a soft, tortured, grunting sound in the back of his throat. 'You see . . .'

He caught her hand. 'Ria, for God's sake have pity, you're going to regret this.' He tried to lift his body away from hers and shuddered as she pushed her hips against him, desperate for him to abandon his control. She used every instinct she had, and some she hadn't known about, to entice him, squirming on the bed so that the nightdress slipped further, baring her breasts completely, raising one knee so that it pressed intimately between his legs. As she slid against him she whispered with soft urgency:

'Please, James, I need you . . .' She bit him, then licked the soft indentations, abandoning all her inhibitions in the raw intensity of the moment. What had begun as a desire to forget had become an overwhelming passion. All the attraction she had felt for James in the past came crashing down on her . . . she wanted him, *now*, with an urgency that was soul-destroying. 'Please, James . . .'

Her voice, full of the agony of wanting, shattered his resistance and suddenly James was no longer fighting the inevitable. His body was lying heavily on hers, crushing her into the bed, his powerful hands cupping her face, holding it still for his burning kisses. His tongue thrust deeply, almost savagely, into her mouth and Ria tasted fire, felt it race through her body.

Biting, kissing, sucking, stroking, he travelled over her body, peeling off her nightdress and his own pyjamas, meshing their bodies together with teasing movements of long, hair-roughened limbs. As his hands skimmed her breasts, Ria gasped frantically, aching for his intimate touch. But he circled the taut mounds, avoiding the stiff centres until Ria was moaning with need. When he did it was like a sword plunged to the core of her womanhood. She cried out when his fingers splayed under her breasts, readying them for his mouth.

His tongue moistly lashed her until she tore his head away and launched feverishly into her own explorations.

James seemed to relish her need to be aggressive, encouraging her passionate assault on his body, watching her through half-closed lids as she pleasured herself with his body. In truth he was incredibly aroused by her hungry boldness, deliberately playing on it, a tiny, sane part of his mind telling him that it would have taken him weeks ... months ... in normal circumstances to get her to trust him enough to be so sexually receptive. It might be unfair to Ria, but he sensed that this was an opportunity to brand for ever on her memory that they were good together. After this she could never deny that he could give her fulfilment. Tonight he would show her that they belonged in each other's arms. Tomorrow he would claim what was his.

Fiercely he devoted himself to his task and at last, when Ria felt she could bear it no longer: 'Now, please, James——' she cried, trying to pull him over her, groaning when he resisted.

'No, Ria, not like that . . .' He kissed her hotly, lifting her up so that her thighs fell over his, holding her hips and lowering her on to him. 'This way, angel . . .' He moaned softly as her thighs fell either side of his and he felt her trembling softness above him. 'Come, Ria,' he enticed thickly,' take what you want . . .'

He gloried in the explosive lack of control that arched her body. Ria threw her head back, shuddering as James manipulated their pleasure, feeling his hands move languidly on her swollen breasts as his hips rotated beneath hers. Then the whirlwind dashed away her heady sense of power, sucking everything inwards for an instant then shattering outwards. Ria fell, sprawling across the hard, masculine body, hot salty tears of release falling from wide, wondering eyes.

Exhausted in mind and body, she fell asleep i his arms, unaware of the man staring into the darkness beside her, ruefully contemplating the novelty of the situation. Usually it was the woman who wanted to talk, the man who fell asleep—or at least in his experience. But he couldn't sleep, he felt too uncertain of what he might find when he woke up. He mustn't let her back down, and he was sure she would try.

Twice more in the night Ria woke in the toils of nightmare, and twice more she lost her fear in the strong, lithe body that was so ready to give and receive pleasure.

The third time she woke it was to see James, showered and shaved and dressed only in a towel flung casually around his hips, sitting on the side of the wide bed.

'Michel——?' Her first word was instinctive.

'The same, I rang a few minutes ago. How are you feeling?'

Suddenly she felt the rasp of the sheet against her naked skin, and the night came rushing back. The blue eyes darkened as they watched the slow blush climb above the sheet.

'James—last night, I——'

'Don't. You. Dare,' he said softly, separating each word explicitly.

'W-what?' Her whole body felt scalded with embarrassment. Why, she had *begged* him to make love to her. She had practically raped him! And he had been so reluctant!

'Say it was a mistake.' He read her mind. 'It wasn't.'

'I—I was using you,' she said awkwardly, looking away. After all her deceptions, she owed him honesty now. She had wanted him, but not just James Everett, she had wanted a *man*.

Incredibly, he smiled. 'I know.' Startled she looked back and was caught in the sensuous blue web. 'I did a little using of my own. I knew you weren't ready for me, Ria, not really, but I let it happen anyway.'

She swallowed at the intent in his eyes.

'So we agree,' he continued gently. 'Last night was for you ... but this morning, this morning is for me.'

He put his hand on her breast and Ria felt her body's shock of recognition.

'James, we mustn't—you have to go to work, and I have to go to the hospital,' she said weakly, appalled at the acuteness of her sensual memory.

'Later.' He tugged at the sheet and pulled it away from her body, looking down at her as she instinctively tried to cover herself. He pulled her hand away from her breasts and a look of sheer delight came over his face. Ria stared, entranced, at the dancing blue lights in his eyes, the curving mouth.

'I couldn't see last night, in the dark,' he murmured, 'but I wondered whether your breasts had freckles over them. I was sure that I could taste them, like sprinkles of brown sugar to sweeten the whipped cream skin.' He lowered his mouth on her. 'Mmmm, they seem to melt in my mouth . . . *you* melt in my mouth, Ria.'

This time there was none of the urgency of the night. This time there were no shadows to drive back, only a dazzling, multi-coloured light behind her eyelids. This time James controlled her eager arousal, alternately stroking her to a peak then holding back until the intensity began to fade, slowly, slowly, building the tension until it reached a climactic pitch. This time he went all the way with her, reinforcing the physical bond with erotic whispers describing his pleasure, wrenching from her the response he sought, he needed.

'You see,' he murmured into her relaxed, passion-washed face when it was over. There was a masculine possessiveness about him that she felt too deliciously languid to deny. 'Whatever the reason we came together last night, this morning proves that we should give it a chance. It feels so good, Ria, to make love to you, so natural.' He closed her mouth with a gentle finger as she opened it to protest. 'I know it's a difficult time for you, so I'm not going to press it. Deep down, you know you trust me, or your subconscious wouldn't have let you give yourself to me the way you did. Trust me enough to look after you while Michel's ill. Stay here

... you and Paul and Jamie. Lean on me, use me, whatever you need, Ria—just don't shut me out. I need to be needed, too, you know.'

CHAPTER TEN

RIA watched Michel march up and down the line of beds in the children's ward, dispensing silly jokes along with his goodbyes. Now that he was better he seemed to have twice the energy he had before.

'I have the strange feeling that it never really happened.' Ria shook her head and smiled at the doctor. 'As if it was all just a bad dream.'

'It's a common reaction,' Dr Bradley assured her, 'especially in cases like Michel's. As I said, there's a lot we still don't know about the brain. Sometimes things seem to happen for no rhyme nor reason that medical science can discover. We must just be grateful for the human body's capacity to heal itself.'

Ten days after the accident Michel had suddenly opened his eyes and demanded food, which he promptly brought straight up again. He had been vague and disorientated, but had not complained of pain. Ria had worried for days that the condition might be permanent but her concern had been needless. Since then Michel had been submitted to a battery of tests and passed with flying colours.

A pale, listless little boy in the end bed giggled at one of Michel's corny jokes. During his four-week stay in hospital Michel had made a number of new friends. Some of them, Ria knew, would never be going home and not a day passed that she didn't give thanks that her son was one of the lucky ones.

In another, more intimate sense, she felt the dreamlike quality of the last month. During the day her thoughts had been focused on her son, but at night her world had narrowed still further, encompassed by her lover's arms. That first, hungry coming-together had smashed the barriers between Ria and James. It had seemed pointless to deny what had happened or to assume a modest reluctance after her eager and uninhibited passion the night before. So the next night, and the next, and every night thereafter, James had come to her bed and she had welcomed him. It became an island, a sanctuary where they shed past and future in the pleasures of the moment. Far from slaking her passion, Ria found that James' lovemaking was like a drug. It heightened her senses, intensified light and colour, touch and taste, and each time it was over she craved more. She had never known such delirium. He was by turns dominant and possessive, passionate and provocative, teasing and tender and Ria loved each new facet as it revealed itself. She loved him fiercely, secretly, without reservation. Time enough later for regrets. For now she grabbed greedily at what she could get.

Paul seemed unsurprised by the change in her relationship with James and his lack of awkwardness further cocooned Ria from the consequences of her actions. She was blindly grateful that no one seemed to be expecting any kind of decision or purposeful action from her . . . she seemed incapable of either. She merely wanted to love . . .

But as Michel got better her lovely dream world began to develop strains; one of them was the twins' reaction to James. They too, had fallen under his spell.

'He's nice,' Jamie had accused her reproachfully on one occasion. 'Nothing like what you said.'

'*And* he knows which one of us is which,' said Michel, with a shy look at his brother. 'Jamie and I switched places yesterday when he came to visit, but Uncle James *knew*.'

'Well, you're a bit thinner than your brother at the moment,' Ria had pointed out hastily, although it was true, James did seem to have an instinct that was beginning to elude the nursing staff. Perversely, Ria found herself resenting it, and the tantalising possibilities it raised.

When, finally, she forced herself to stand back and look at the impossible situation she had got herself into she felt the first clawings of panic. James never talked about his feelings. It was as though he were deliberately holding back from her. Oh, he quite openly expressed desire, and seemed to enjoy Ria's company, but he never talked about what would happen when Michel got well. Was he waiting for her to make the first move? She didn't dare. Try as she might she no longer had the ability to read him the way she had been able to when she was just his secretary. Love got in the way. She couldn't come out with a flat statement that she was in love with him, not without preparing the way first. It had never been a possibility . . . at least as far as James was concerned, not after what he'd said about marriage. For marriage read love; he wasn't ready for that, yet, either.

He would probably be embarrassed if she blurted out her feelings. He might pity her, recoil in distaste. Perhaps he was expecting her to suggest leaving, so that they could both bow out of the affair gracefully. Now that Michel was better she had no excuse for staying. Perhaps James would suggest some other kind of arrangement. Ria went cold at the thought of formalising her position as his mistress. Yet the alternative was even more chilling. Did she have the strength to make a clean break? She didn't know, she feared not . . . a little piece of James was better than nothing at all.

Ria shivered as she shepherded Michel out of the hospital. This morning she had finally plucked up the courage to test the waters, and had almost drowned in the attempt.

James had been knotting his tie in front of the mirror when she entered his bedroom. He had smiled at her, his blue eyes warm with the memory of the way he had left her. Could he look like that and still want to break off the affair? Ria felt ill with the nervous tension. She loved the way his eyes slanted at her, the hard angles of his face and the arrogant nose. She loved the thick, black hair that felt so soft and warm in her hands. She loved everything about him ... and he was going to hurt her, horribly. The sudden certainty rushed her into speech.

'James ... after I've picked up Michel I think we'll go home. It's time we moved back. You've been marvellous to put up with us all, but ...' Her confidence crumbled even further as he turned slowly, his fingers stilling on the knot, the smile stilled on his face. Oh God, it had come out all wrong. Too formal, too grateful.

'*Put up* with you, Ria? Is that all I've been doing? How disappointing for you.'

Ria felt the band around her throat tighten at the faint mockery in the unrevealing response. Dear God, wasn't he even going to make a *token* protest? 'I—The doctor said to keep him home from school for another week, but to get him back into his normal routine as soon as possible. She said that after all the attention he's been getting, he'll probably be extra demanding for a while.'

Her eyes were everywhere but on James' face, so she missed the sudden narrowing of his eyes when she said 'normal'.

'When do you plan on coming back to work?' he asked quietly.

She cleared her throat. 'I thought ... when Michel goes back to school. If that's all right with you,' she added hurriedly. 'I know I've had a lot of time off already, but it's just another week. 'I ... I don't want to be paid or anything ...' The practicalities suddenly occurred to her. 'Have I been on holiday these past weeks, or——'

She was cut off by the harsh sound in his throat. 'Damn you, Ria, do you realise what an insult that is?'

Belatedly she did, and it tied her up into worse knots. 'I'm sorry, I didn't mean ...' she floundered while he watched in ominous silence. If she had been thinking clearly she would have been worried by his quietness, but she was so conscious of the mess she was making of her carefully planned speech that she couldn't even bear to contemplate the impression she was making.

'So you want everything back to normal,' he said finally, in a precise, controlled voice. 'Are you trying to tell me, in your roundabout way, that what we've been doing for the past few weeks is *abnormal*?'

It registered then, and she looked him full in the face for the first time. He looked too calm, not a muscle moving in his face. His eyes were hard and cold, so cold . . .

She went to spread her hands and then changed her mind, they were shaking so much. She clasped them behind her instead. 'Well—I—if Michel hadn't had his accident we wouldn't have . . .'

'Made love? Don't kid yourself, Ria. It just happened sooner, that's all. We would have become lovers anyway.'

She couldn't deny it. But why did he say it with such contempt? If he wanted her to stay, why didn't he take her in his arms and tell her so, smother her protests with his lovemaking? They both knew he could.

'I can't stay here, James, you must see that,' she insisted desperately, wishing he wouldn't stare at her so as if he was willing her to say . . . what?

'Are you worried what people might think? It's a bit late for that, isn't it?'

It had never even occurred to her. 'Not people, but . . . there's Jamie and Michel. I don't want them to think——' That you're a permanent fixture in their lives, she wanted to say, but if she mentioned permanency he might feel she was trying to pressure him into committing himself further than he wanted to go. She wanted to avoid that at all costs.

'What? That they've got competition?' His voice dropped so low she could hardly hear it, but the blistering emphasis was carried by tone alone. 'That you actually exist outside their little world? Heaven forbid that Mummy should be unfaithful!'

'James!' Ria felt shocked by the bitter undercurrent, by the confirmation that he tolerated the twins only because he had to. Although she had prepared herself she still felt the deep, ripping pain. 'It isn't like that . . . but Michel's going to need special attention for a while, I won't have time——'

'For a lover?' he supplied, cold as a knife. He bent and picked up his jacket from the bed, shouldering into it with a suppressed violence that shredded Ria's exposed nerves. 'You have it all worked out, don't you? And the hell with what anyone else wants . . . Ria is back in charge. I suppose you've been rehearsing this little scene all night. Was that why you were so delightfully responsive last night . . . softening me up for the *coup de grâce*?'

Ria flinched, knowing he had reason for the sneering assumption. Last night she had been excruciatingly aware that it might be the last night they had together. She had been wild and wanton, saying with her mouth and hands and body what she was afraid to say in words.

He saw her flinch and it was a savage backhand to his pride, to all his hopes. 'You bitch,' he enunciated softly. 'And to think I actually believed you were finally letting me in, not planning to slam the door in my face.'

'James, don't——' she choked. What did he mean, 'letting him in'? She had never denied him in bed, hadn't been able to; whatever he had wanted she had tried to give.

'I suppose you thought you could manipulate me at will!' His blue eyes blazed contempt and suddenly he abandoned his quiet fury, exploding forth in raw accusation. 'Did you think that because you were good in bed I'd forgive you anything? You didn't lie when you said you were using me, did you? Only I didn't realise quite how completely. You were quite happy to run crying to me for comfort in a crisis, quite happy to trust me to take care of you, of your family, quite happy for me to supply you with sex-on-demand. But that's as far as it goes, isn't it, Angel Mouth?' The insult was made doubly corrosive by the nickname he had been wont to use when they were making love. 'Now that your little circle is complete again you want to retreat within its nice and tidy perimeter. Well, what if I'm not ready to let you go, Ria? What if I want you in my bed a bit longer? Another week should do it ... there are one or two variations we haven't tried yet.'

Ria felt as if he was cutting out her heart. She recognised that it was anger that made him so vicious, but she died a little as she realised its source. He resented the thought that she might want to end their affair. His pride was hurt. *He* must be the one to decide when an affair had run its course.

'I have to go——' she mumbled, acid tears burning at the back of her throat, turning to flee like a wounded animal.

He caught her. 'Not before you say goodbye properly.' He wrenched her around and smiled insolently at her pale face.

She swayed on her feet as she realised what he meant. '*No*! James——' She pushed at him.

'Gone off it, Ria? You couldn't get enough of it last night.' He stripped her with his eyes.

'Just my way of saying thanks,' she stabbed at him blindly, and heard his low hiss as the words found their mark.

'Gratitude, Ria?' His hands bit into her hips as he thrust himself against her. 'Oh no, I won't let you hide behind that one. You slept with me because you couldn't help yourself. You weren't faking, you were crazy for me.'

'You arrogant bastard.' Ria defended herself against the truth, terrified of what he would make her admit.

'Is it arrogant for a man to know when he's giving a woman pleasure?' His breath was hot on her face as his fingers wound themselves into her hair, his eyes like lasers probing an open wound. 'Is it arrogant of me to assume that when you're lying under me shaking and groaning and sobbing about how good I make you feel that you're telling the truth? You lying bitch, you enjoy it, don't you, *don't you*?'

'That's just lust,' she gasped trying to avoid the radiating heat that the hard body was transmitting to every pore.

'*Just* lust?' He gave a grating laugh as he felt her shudder. 'Baby, it's not *just* anything.' For a brief, heady instant she thought he was going to say more, to tell her what they shared was more than sex, that it touched his mind and spirit also. Tell me, she cried silently against the tears, make me tell *you*. But his torture was relentless.

'We still want each other, Ria,' he said hoarsely, 'however much you try to pretend otherwise. Let me show you how much . . .'

He took one of the hands pressed against his chest and drew it down against the dark fabric of his trousers. Ria tried to pull away, to deny the purely physical arousal she felt pulsing against her palm. His was a dark and angry passion and she feared its forceful attraction.

'See what you do to me,' he groaned and in a blind riot of sensation she felt him move himself against her, his other hand sliding across her stomach to push against her skirt, cupping her intimately between the thighs.

'And I do it to you, Angel Mouth . . .' he said thickly. His fingers flexed and Ria felt a hot, humiliating rush of desire. Her knees sagged and she almost fell. 'See . . . you don't really want to go . . .'

They were the wrong words. If he had said 'I don't want you to go' she would have given in, helpless to fight his need. But he hadn't, he was trying to make her betray herself. She suffered his hot, hard kiss, felt his anger bruising her lips, and she twisted and fell back.

'No! You think that just because you can make me feel like *that* I should give in to it?' She laughed wildly.

'It's not enough and it never will be. You don't begin to know what I need, and even if you did you couldn't give it to me.' A dark red streak rose above his cheekbones but the glittering, ice-blue eyes never left hers. 'I belong to my sons, and they belong to me, and nothing, no one, is going to change that. They come first with me, always. I won't sacrifice love for sex, not ever.'

She cried when he had gone, stiff, wordless, all fire and anger wiped away by her passionate sincerity. Only he hadn't really understood what she was saying and she was too afraid to tell him. She meant what she said about the boys coming first, but what she hadn't said was that it didn't have to be a choice. That there was always room for more love in her life. That the love she felt for him, James, was as strong in its way as her love for her sons.

Oh, God, her foolish words had destroyed so much! She should have risked being honest. She should have remembered his gentleness, his caring, all the small, shared experiences that had tempered the lovemaking. She should have trusted him enough to give him the chance.

The tears stung her face. *I need to be needed too*, he had said that first morning in her arms. And she had taunted him with her family's self-sufficiency. With a lie. Wasn't needing part of being loved? Had he been asking if she could love him?

She felt so confused. All the next week she conducted arguments with herself. Alone in her single bed, longing for his warmth, she could believe that there was still a germ of hope, that they could work things out if she opened up to him and showed him the true depths of her feelings. In daylight, coping with an active and sometimes fractious Michel, she despaired. Why would he want to take on her burdens? Even if he did love her, a little, in return, what would it mean? Back to square one—an affair?

She wavered, uncertain, despising herself for the uncertainty. When the time came to go back to work she still hadn't decided what to do, what attitude to take.

From the moment she stepped inside the office she could feel the arctic atmosphere—James Everett at his most Olympian. Ria felt she had walked into a time machine, his detachment was so complete. She no longer existed as a separate entity, she was an extension of his desk again. As she sat and took the first morning's dictation she bled silently, invisibly, all over the beautiful grey carpet. Nothing would change in the office, he had said, and nothing had. They had made love and ripped each other to shreds, but Everett Communications didn't care.

Sometimes, over the next fortnight, Ria thought she detected a flicker of humanity beneath the perma-frost but it was probably wishful thinking. She tried hard to match his cold indifference but it was a losing battle. Inside she was screaming. Twice attractive women, whom Ria had never seen before, arrived without an appointment and were taken out to lunch. Each time Ria had been physically ill with the force of her jealous emotion. He was doing it deliberately, she thought. Was he trying to force her into handing in her resignation? She would see him in hell first! If he wanted to get rid of her he would have to come out in the open and fire her, and she would have him in court so fast his feet wouldn't touch the ground! Loving him and hating him at the same time was exhausting, yet at the same time exhilarating. She felt like an explosion waiting for someone to light the fuse, and she willed James to strike the match.

If she had but known it, her mere presence was putting her tormentor on the rack. She looked so composed. Even the sight of him with another woman hadn't put a dent in her smooth exterior. She had even smiled slightly. He had wanted to smash that smile off her face. He wanted to make violent love to her, he wanted her to throw herself at him so he could reject her as cruelly and categorically as she had rejected him.

James' jaw ached from clenching his teeth. It seemed to him that Ria smiled at every man but him. He had to physically restrain himself from ripping out Gerry's throat every time his assistant made a flirtatious remark. And Ria responded, as if she had never lain in James' arms and gasped out her pleasure against his chest. Damn her, how could a woman be so soft and vulnerable yet so hard and unyielding? He spent endless hours trying to devise her downfall, grimly avoiding the answer that lay in the deepest, darkest shadows of his psyche.

Fortunately for the self-control of the silent protagonists, there came a cease-fire. James flew down to Wellington to present Everett Communications' application for a private television broadcasting licence. As well as presenting the submission to the Broadcasting Tribunal, James would be attending a number of other business meetings and would be away for an entire working week. Just before he left, he and Ria spoke their first civil words to each other in a fortnight.

After issuing her with a curt list of tasks for her to fulfil in his absence James had paused and said suddenly, as if driven, 'It's not working, is it, Ria?'

Startled, she looked quickly away. 'No.' There was defeat in the admission. She couldn't go on like this, it was too much of a strain . . . especially now.

'Do you want to leave?'

She met a bleak, wintry gaze. He didn't look triumphant, he looked merely tired. Ria's heart felt like a dead weight in her chest. It was too late now to try and right past wrongs, far too late. She nodded.

His lids came down, shuttering his face still further. He rolled a pen on his blotter. 'I hate to lose a good secretary but as far as working for me is concerned, you're right.' Ria's eyes blurred and she missed the travesty of a smile. 'Life is obviously not as tidy as we both hoped it would be. Leave it with me. I'll find something in one of the other companies . . . I'll make sure you won't lose by it.'

'But I don't——'

'I can do that much at least!' he said, with a violence that was at odds with his weariness. 'You have two children to support and you still have the rest of that mortgage to pay off. You can't toss in a high-paying job simply because of . . . personal conflicts.'

Two children to support? Inside Ria was dying. If only he knew—and he would have to, some time. But not yet. First she had to get used to the idea, to work out what she was going to do.

The nausea, the tenderness in her breasts, her being overdue—it should have sunk in sooner. After all, she had been pregnant before! Perhaps she didn't want to face the appalling truth until she had to, but there was no getting away from it. The morning sickness had become marked. She was going to have James' child!

There was no question of not having it. She never considered that, even in the first, appalled realisation. She saw her comfortable life dissolving around her . . . a lifetime's reminder of a disastrous love affair. She saw pain, embarrassment, humiliation. She saw herself going cap in hand to James . . .

But when the trapped, panicky feeling had passed Ria felt a strange complacency steal over her. James' baby. It had a sweetly possessive sound. Childbirth held no fears for her, nor motherhood itself. The tiny life inside her had been created out of love, just as much as her other children. Perhaps her total abrogation of responsibility during a month of lovemaking had been a subconscious attempt to forge just such a link between James and herself. So that whatever happened, however far apart they were, she would always have something of him, a remnant of love grafted from his own body.

It meant, of course, that she could never, now, tell James that she loved him. He wouldn't believe it. Child support—he said himself that was all a pregnant mistress could expect. It was all she would ask for. And there would be no attempt at excuses this time. She would tell him baldly that she wanted the baby and intended to have it, and that she could not afford to bring it up on her own.

It was difficult enough breaking the news to Paul, but she felt she owed it to him to warn him as soon as possible. He had been stunned, but in his typically realistic fashion had approached the difficulties matter-of-factly. Only when it came to James did he and Ria differ.

'I don't think you should make any decisions at all until you've discussed it with him. The baby is his, Ria, as much as yours.'

'He's already told me he's not interested in fatherhood.' Ria lashed herself with the knowledge.

'In general terms, perhaps. But a man feels differently when the child is his. He did not strike me, *chérie*, as a man to shirk responsibility.'

'I don't just want to be a responsibility,' Ria cried.

'Does that mean that if he offers marriage you will refuse?'

'He won't,' she replied grimly. 'But if he does, it would be unfair to accept.'

'Unfair to whom?' persisted Paul. 'What about this child? Will you deny it anything other than a "sometime" father? And what about Jamie and Michel? What happens when they realise that the new brother or sister has a father that you have denied *them*?'

He raised all kinds of questions that were too painful to think about. His logic made Ria angry and self-pitying. It was so tempting, to persuade herself that she should trap James into marriage for the sake of the children. But that would be using them as an excuse, when the real reason she wanted to marry him was because she loved him, and didn't want to live without him. But she couldn't tell him that. It was a vicious circle and there seemed no escape . . .

James arrived back from Wellington on Friday, but didn't come into the office at all and Ria was grateful for the reprieve. She had enough to cope with. The boys had overheard a conversation between her and Paul, and were now privy to the new arrival far sooner than she had wanted them to be. No doubt in a few days the novelty would wear off, especially when they realised that the baby would not be born for months yet and even then wouldn't be able to walk or talk or join in their games. There'd be jealousy, too, to cope with, and the awkward questions that were bound to arise as the pregnancy began to show. It didn't occur to them right now that anyone else might be involved with the baby's intrusion into their world, but the question of a daddy was sure to be voiced one day.

On Saturday morning the nausea was so bad that Paul insisted she stay home while he took the twins to soccer. Tony had promised to go along to watch, too, since his school had a later game on the same pitch, so Jamie and Michel would not be lacking for an extra supporter.

Ria lay in bed, sipping weak tea and nibbling crackers, until she felt able to move about without the floor rocking beneath her. At half-past ten she was in the kitchen, still in her robe, when the doorbell rang.

It was James Everett.

He looked fit and well-rested and stunningly attractive in grey slacks and a pink and grey cotton-knit sweater. He was holding an enormous sheaf of roses, a spectacular marmalade colour. Ria stared at them dumbly. How like James to be obscure. What in the hell did marmalade roses mean? *Transferred to the Wellington office*, perhaps? She glared at him.

'May I come in?'

She felt dreadful and knew she looked. it. Her face was pale and there were circles under her eyes. Her hair felt limp and as lifeless as she did.

She stood back reluctantly and followed him into the kitchen. She had forgotten he had been here before, when she was at the hospital.

'Shall I put these in water for you?' he asked pleasantly, his face composed into unrevealing lines.

'I . . .' She wanted to snatch the roses and bury her haggard face in their blazing beauty but her stomach was suddenly acting up again.

'Is this a vase?' He took one down from the sill, seeming unconcerned by her lack of enthusiasm. He filled it from the tap and placed the roses in it, arranging them quite handily before carrying the whole over to the kitchen table.

'Th-thank you,' Ria stammered, wrenching her hungry eyes away from his back as he turned towards her.

'They reminded me of you,' he said quietly, blue eyes unwavering. 'Such a distinctive colouring, such a heady perfume, and so beautiful that it's easy to forget about those thorns. See?' He held out a finger and showed her a tiny pinprick of blood. Ria was devastated by sweeping desire. She wanted to cradle his hand in hers and kiss the blood away.

'W-why are you here?' she asked jerkily as James leaned against the kitchen table, leaving her exposed in the centre of the floor. He looked different—relaxed, almost happy. Ria wondered, stricken, whether he had met someone in Wellington who made him look like this.

'I thought perhaps it was time we talked on your territory, since we don't seem to get very far on mine. And I knew you'd be on your own. I went down to watch the soccer for a while, with Tony.'

'To watch the twins?' Ria stared at him, assailed by creeping tension.

'Why not?' He smiled wryly at her surprise. 'I promised them I would. If you weren't so busy trying to protect the twins from me, and me from the twins, you would have found out we get on rather well.'

'I wasn't doing that,' she said quickly. 'Well, maybe a little—' when he continued to regard her steadily. It was exactly what she *had* done, she realised. She had been afraid that if the twins bothered him too much he would tire of her more quickly, but was also afraid of them getting too close. 'I suppose I was a bit jealous,' she admitted stiffly.

'Jealous?' He pounced. 'Of your own sons?'

Sensitive to his incredulity she backed off, but he looked pleased at her stumble into reluctant honesty. 'I . . . well, you're all *males*,' she said helplessly. 'You . . . have this . . . rapport——' She felt foolish admitting it, afraid of how much it revealed.

'You feel stupid, don't you, admitting that you're jealous of a child? Imagine how *I* felt about Tony! Imagine how *I* felt about resenting natural maternal affection. It rattles all sorts of skeletons.'

He was being gentle, he was raising hopes he had no right to. Ria turned away and staggered to the bench. She felt moisture beginning to break out in little pearls all over her body. She clenched her teeth, trying to fight the rising tide of sickness; it was all a matter of mental control. Please, please don't let me disgrace myself in front of James, she thought. Not like this. Not when they had just begun to communicate.

'Ria? Are you all right?' He was by her side instantly, his touch on her elbow adding to the sickness.

'I . . . I'm not feeling too good. That's why I didn't go to soccer,' she said through her teeth. 'I must be coming down with something.'

The cerulean eyes darkened. 'Rather a casual way to dismiss our child, don't you think, Ria?'

'Oh!'

The rush of horror, of relief, breached the barriers of her control. She leaned over, clinging miserably to the sink as she retched.

'Please, go away——' she found the strength to gasp, humiliated by James' firm, gentle bracing of her heaving shoulders.

'Ssshhh, it's all right.' His soothing words reminded her of that night when gentleness had turned to raging desire. He held her until she finished, then ran the tap in the sink, dampening his handkerchief and softly patting her face with its blessed coolness.

'I think you'd better sit down. I'll get you a glass of water.'

He sat down beside her, grave and quiet, as she sipped.

'Did Paul . . .?'

'Close as the grave. No, it was Jamie and Michel. They came over to see me at half-time—they were winning by the way, three-one, when I left—and they couldn't wait to tell me about their new baby. They want a girl, by the way, but only if she's not a sissy.'

'Oh God.' Ria closed her eyes. 'I really didn't mean them to know, but they overheard——'

'And me, Ria? When did you mean me to know? I'm presuming, of course, that I *am* the father.'

Her eyes flew open. 'Of course you are!'

Now that he had her pinned down, he wouldn't let her look away. 'When were you going to tell me?'

She moistened her lips from the glass. 'I . . . eventually . . .'

He expelled a breath, his eyes glittering dangerously. 'Eventually?' Why? Did you think I wouldn't want you to have it, that I'd ask you to have an abortion?'

'No!' She was shocked. 'I wouldn't anyway . . . I just didn't know how to tell you. I was going to wait until I'd been to a doctor.'

'You mean you aren't sure yet?' He frowned.

'Of course I am . . . I have been through this before, you know.'

'But *I* haven't.' He was still frowning. 'Are you going to go soon? Will it be all right . . . at your age . . . I mean——'

'I'm not over the hill yet,' she declared, offended by the suggestion.

'Not by a long chalk, darling,' he drawled, and she flushed, suddenly angry again at his mocking grin.

'It's easy for you to joke about it——' she began hotly, but he interrupted her abruptly.

'It's not easy at all, Ria, especially since I can imagine all the plans you've been busily making in my absence.'

'I don't know what you mean,' she denied.

'Liar! I bet you were going to be terribly businesslike about it, maybe you were even going to suggest drawing up papers—you know, assuring me that you wouldn't expect anything other than minimal financial support. Nothing for yourself, of course. And God forbid that I should actually want to do anything crass like propose that we make the baby legitimate.'

Ria looked down at her fingers, curling defensively around the glass, holding on to cool, transparent reality.

'You obviously remembered every word I said about not getting trapped into marriage. Did you forget what I said about contraception?

She felt the lightest touch on her cheek, like the brush of a butterfly wing. She slanted soft, tear-stung eyes sideways to see James leaning towards her, with such a tender expression on his face that she quivered inside.

'I said I was quite willing to take care of it myself. I had the means, Ria, I just didn't use them. It's not me who's trapped, darling, it's you. Will you forgive me?' He smiled crookedly as if he was half-afraid of her reaction.

Ria could hardly speak for the obstruction in her throat. Her head was pounding with the implications— 'You ... *wanted* me to get pregnant?'

'Let's just say the thought crossed my mind and wasn't rejected.'

'But ... but you let me go!' The whole, awful argument came back to mock his words.

'My temper sometimes gets the better of me,' he admitted with a small gesture of his hands. Ria blinked. They were trembling. She looked at the wry twist of his mouth. It was uncertain. 'I had no idea what was going on inside your head ... I thought we had reached a kind of tacit understanding and suddenly there you were, trotting out all the old excuses. I blew my top. And then, when you were so cold in the office, I thought I'd really lost you.'

So *cold*? Ria stared at him in disbelief.

'I didn't know how to approach you again. My pride refused to beg. I had decided to start all over again. While I was away I thought: this time we'll do it properly, this time I'll woo her.' His voice deepened. 'Then, when the twins blurted out your little secret my first thought was: Thank God, now I don't have to wait.'

'James——' she whispered helplessly. Was he still talking about wanting? Whatever, she couldn't deny her love a second time.

'Sitting down there in that lonely hotel I realised how bloody awful my life would be without you. I don't care if I have to share you with the world, Ria . . . I realised that, too. I thought . . . if I'm afraid to tell her that I love her, perhaps she is, too—especially after all those stupid things I said about marriage. Because you are the marrying kind, aren't you, Ria?'

She was terrified of moving. If she moved she felt this delicate dream would shatter.

'Ria . . .' He stood up, and drew her up with him. His hand slid down to her stomach, fingers of fire splayed against the thin robe. 'That's part of me inside you. It awes me, it excites me, makes me feel so . . . strange. Oh, Ria, I want to watch your belly swell with my child. I want to feel her kicking against her confinement, I want to hold you when you hurt, I want to share the miracle of her birth.' His hand soothed over her stomach and Ria leant her head against his shoulder with a whispered moan. 'Will you share her with me, Ria? Will you share some of your love with me in exchange for all of mine? Just give me a chance to show you that I can make you happy.'

'You already have,' she said, and the arm around her tightened involuntarily.

'I haven't even begun,' he murmured into her hair. He leaned back, to read her eyes and his skin reddened at what he saw. 'Will you love my child as much as you love Jamie and Michel?' His eyes dropped as his hand came up to caress her breasts through the silky robe. His voice hoarsened. 'Will you feed her yourself, let her suckle at your breast as you let me?'

Ria shivered with loving desire. 'I'll love her as much as I love you.' She gave him the reassurance, sensing that he would always need to have it emphasised, freely and often.

He cupped her face with his hands and kissed her hungrily. 'Thank God.' And then, more sternly, 'Why did you try so hard to push me away, Ria?'

'I thought all you wanted was an affair and I didn't think you were the kind of man who'd want to take on a ready-made family.'

His face tautened. 'I didn't think so myself . . . until I got to know you and the twins. But I love you, Ria, the whole of you, not just selected bits.' He stopped to kiss her, then began again. 'You knocked me for six, my little counterfeit secretary. One minute you were simply an office fixture, the next you had me climbing the walls. You were so deliciously mysterious. And then, when I began uncovering the mystery I found you even more deliciously complex.'

'Were you angry, when you found out about the twins?' she asked, not remembering very much about those hazy days.

He gave her the smallest of shakes. 'Later, but at the time I was too stunned to be anything. All my preconceptions about you were in tatters. A mother? I felt cheated of something. Dismayed at how jealous I felt when you were going through agonies and I didn't have the right to be there with you. I was nobody.'

'James Everett, nobody?' She laughed shakily at the image.

'Mmm.' He ran his hands over her body to reassure himself that she was still there. 'That's when I realised that I loved you. But instead of making everything simple it made things that much more difficult. I couldn't think logically any more—I found myself resenting your family for having known and loved you before me. I was glad when you turned to me that night. I thought I could bind you to me with sex, if nothing else. And that later you would realise how much all the other things mattered—the caring, the friendship. I thought I could make you love me by making you reliant on me. I should have given you the words, I know, but I was scared to death that it would be too soon for you. That I'd frighten you off. You seemed so vulnerable but I knew that inside you were tempered steel—used to facing things on your own, without me. When you told me you were leaving it was like my worst nightmare coming true. I loved you and hated you at the same time.'

'Oh, how I know that feeling.' Ria smiled at him, green eyes deep and drowning in loving tears.

'I can be a brute when I try, can't I?'

'That, Mr Everett, is an understatement,' she said severely. 'All I wanted you to do was take me in your arms and tell me you loved me and never wanted me to go.'

'If only I had,' he groaned, inhaling the fragrance from the hollow of her throat. 'God how I missed you! I even missed Jamie and Michel because they were part of you, part of what I loved. That's what made me realise that I had nothing to be jealous of. Love doesn't exist in isolation, it's like ink on blotting paper, it seeps all over the place.' He hesitated. 'Do you mind, Ria, about the baby? It's terribly selfish of me to be glad about it, but I am. It's another bond, you see, and I'm insecure enough to need every one I can get.'

'That's lucky,' Ria teased, flinging her arms around his neck and moving her body provocatively against his. Her eyes sparkled at him, erasing the slight shadow of doubt in the beautiful blue eyes. 'Because it might be twins. Identical twins are hereditary, you know, not an accident of conception, and there were none on René's side of the family.'

James looked startled for an instant, then his mouth

curved contentedly. 'Two little girls? Perfect, then Michel and Jamie can have a baby sister each. And *you*, Ria Duncan Masson Everett, you can have *me*.'

Harlequin Presents

Coming Next Month

927 AN ELUSIVE MISTRESS Lindsay Armstrong
An interior designer from Brisbane finally finds a man to share the rest of her life with—only to have her ex-husband return and reawaken feelings she'd thought were hidden forever.

928 ABODE OF PRINCES Jayne Bauling
In mysterious Rajasthan, Fate prompts a young woman to redefine her understanding of love and friendship. But the man she meets and loves will hear nothing of her breaking her engagement for him.

929 POPPY GIRL Jaqueline Gilbert
Dreams of wealth don't overwhelm a prospective heiress. But a certain Frenchman does. If only she didn't come to suspect his motives for sweeping her off her feet.

930 LOVE IS A DISTANT SHORE Claire Harrison
A reporter with a knack for getting to the heart of the matter disturbs the concentration of a young woman planning to swim Lake Ontario. Surely she should concentrate on one goal at a time.

931 CAPABLE OF FEELING Penny Jordan
In sharing a roof to help care for her boss's niece and nephew, a young woman comes to terms with her inability to express love. Is it too late to change the confines of their marriage agreement?

932 VILLA IN THE SUN Marjorie Lewty
Villa Favorita is the private paradise she shared with her husband—until his fortunes plummeted and he drove her away. Now she has been asked to handle the sale. Little does she know how closely her husband follows the market.

933 LAND OF THUNDER Annabel Murray
The past is a blank to this accident victim. She feels a stranger to her "husband." Worse, their new employer touches something disturbing within her. Something's terribly wrong here.

934 THE FINAL PRICE Patricia Wilson
In Illyaros, where her Greek grandfather lies ill, her ex-husband denies both their divorce and her right to remarry. Yet he was unfaithful to her! No wonder she hasn't told him about the birth of their son.

Available in November wherever paperback books are sold, or through Harlequin Reader Service:

In the U.S.
P.O. Box 1397
Buffalo, N.Y.
14240-1397

In Canada
P.O. Box 2800, Postal Station A
5170 Yonge Street
Willowdale, Ontario M2N 6J3

Janet Dailey
Americana

Don't miss a single title from this great collection. The first eight titles have already been published. Complete and mail this coupon today to order books you may have missed.

Harlequin Reader Service

In U.S.A.
901 Fuhrmann Blvd.
P.O. Box 1397
Buffalo, N.Y. 14140

In Canada
P.O. Box 2800
Postal Station A
5170 Yonge Street
Willowdale, Ont. M2N 6J3

Please send me the following titles from the Janet Dailey Americana Collection. I am enclosing a check or money order for $2.75 for each book ordered, plus 75¢ for postage and handling.

_____	ALABAMA	Dangerous Masquerade
_____	ALASKA	Northern Magic
_____	ARIZONA	Sonora Sundown
_____	ARKANSAS	Valley of the Vapours
_____	CALIFORNIA	Fire and Ice
_____	COLORADO	After the Storm
_____	CONNECTICUT	Difficult Decision
_____	DELAWARE	The Matchmakers

Number of titles checked @ $2.75 each =	$_____	
N.Y. RESIDENTS ADD APPROPRIATE SALES TAX	$_____	
Postage and Handling	$ .75	
TOTAL	$_____	

I enclose _____

(Please send check or money order. We cannot be responsible for cash sent through the mail.)

PLEASE PRINT

NAME _____

ADDRESS _____

CITY _____

STATE/PROV. _____

BLJD-A-1

Here's how to get this special offer from Harlequin!

✂ October
BETTY NEELS TREASURY EDITION COUPON

As simple as 1...2...3!

1. Each month, save one Treasury Edition coupon from your favorite Romance or Presents novel.
2. In four months you'll have saved four Treasury Edition coupons (only one coupon per month allowed).
3. Then all you have to do is fill out and return the order form provided, along with the four Treasury Edition coupons required and $2.95 for postage and handling.

Mail to: Harlequin Reader Service

In the U.S.A.	In Canada
901 Fuhrmann Blvd.	P.O. Box 609
P.O. Box 1397	Fort Erie, Ontario
Buffalo, NY 14240	L2A 9Z9

BN-Oct-2

Please send me my Special copy of the Betty Neels Treasury Edition. I have enclosed the four Treasury Edition coupons required and $2.95 for postage and handling along with this order form. (Please Print)

NAME_____

ADDRESS_____

CITY_____

STATE/PROV._____ ZIP/POSTAL CODE_____

SIGNATURE_____

This offer is limited to one order per household.

This special Betty Neels offer expires
February 28, 1987.

SUPPLIES LIMITED

Take 4 novels and a surprise gift FREE